# THE BLACK SENTRY

# THE BLACK SENTRY

WILLIAM BERNHARDT

The Black Sentry

First Edition

Copyright © 2014 William Bernhardt Writing Programs

Published by Babylon Books

eBook ISBN: 978-0-9993420-1-5

Paperback ISBN: 978-0-9893789-5-6

*For Ralph, artist and animal lover,*
*our family is so much better because of you*

"Never doubt that a small group of thoughtful, committed citizens can change the world. Indeed, it is the only thing that ever has."

Margaret Mead

# PART ONE

## THE LEAVETAKING

CHAPTER

# ONE

Daman gripped the winnower tightly in his hands, knowing that how he handled it would determine the rest of his life.

He stared into the face of the enemy, barely five feet away, eyes narrowed, lips thin, his own winnower poised and ready to strike. Soon the battle would begin. And it would not end until one of them was finished.

Sweat greased his palms, loosening his grip. He wanted to set the winnower down and wipe his hands dry. But just as he considered it, he heard the doleful sound of the commencement gong. There was no time now. No time for anything.

His enemy smiled.

The best strategy, as he had been told dozens of times, was to take the offensive, to strike first. But he found himself unable to move. His feet felt riveted to the red-dyed stone beneath him. His enemy leapt forward the instant the gong sounded, remaining on his own yellow-colored portion of the Arena floor, but edging as near to his opponent as possible. He held nothing back.

The enemy never did.

The enemy took a swipe at him, blade end out. Fortunately, he stood far enough away to avoid it. The winnower whistled in front of his face, missing him by inches. The winnower was about four feet long. On one end was a round and cone-shaped bulb, solid enough to stun but not to cut. Combatants used it to batter and pummel, or for a quick jab to the stomach. The other end was a sharp fan-shaped blade. A swipe across the neck or through the gut could be fatal.

His enemy changed grip, tucking in the sharp end and swinging the bulb around like a club. He saw it coming. He sprang backwards—though not quickly enough. The bulb battered him on the shoulder, knocking him to his knees.

He tried to scramble to his feet, favoring his injured left arm. He still had time to do something. If he only knew what that might be.

He checked the red intertwined paths, desperately seeking an opening. The Arena was a large octagonal grid. The floor of the grid was divided into intersecting parts, half red and half yellow. Each combatant was required to remain on his color. To step onto an enemy's color resulted in an immediate penalty: the enemy was permitted free run of the entire grid for one turn of the glass, while the transgressor was still restricted to his own color. Rarely could anyone survive such an enormous disadvantage.

He saw another swipe of his enemy's winnower coming, this time low. He leapt up into the air. The winnower whooshed beneath him.

He had to keep moving. If he took another hit, it would be the end. The end of everything.

*Concentrate*, he told himself. You can do this. You must do this.

Everything depends upon it.

Gritting his teeth, he lunged forward, winnower first. His

enemy parried his blow easily, then followed with an extra rapid-fire thrust.

He struggled to retain his grip, falling forward. He lost his balance and almost tumbled onto his enemy's color. Flailing wildly, he stopped himself at the last possible instant, jabbing his winnower into the ground. But the temporary loss of control left him vulnerable. A moment later, he felt the harsh thud of a bulb slamming into the side of his head.

That hurt like nothing he had ever experienced before. His eyes watered. He rolled onto the red, trying to crawl back to a safe place. But he knew no place would remain safe for long. Even as he struggled to catch his breath, his enemy scurried around the grid, zigzagging down the yellow path.

He whipped around, jabbing low with his winnower. For once, his enemy was surprised. The stick caught between his legs and he tripped, spilling headfirst toward the ground.

*Yes.* Now if he'll just fall into the red . . .

But his enemy was too smart and too nimble. Even after losing his balance, his enemy displayed superb reflexes and extraordinary athletic skill. As he fell, he executed a perfect midair forward flip and landed on his feet—still standing on the yellow. Without waiting another instant, the enemy whirled around and battered him on the front of his face.

His head exploded. Blood spurted from his nose. The whole grid spun around him, whirling in fuzzy red and yellow circles.

Hardly a heartbeat later, his enemy pressed the winnower hard against his throat.

This was more than defeat. This was complete humiliation.

"It's done," his enemy said, his voice harsh and direct. "Your life is over."

# TWO

Daman found himself unable to speak. His head swam and his thoughts collided. He felt barely conscious, gasping for air.

"That's it, then," his enemy said, still pressing the winnower to his neck. "You're dead, or you're a grunt for the rest of your life, which amounts to the same thing. Which would you prefer?"

He felt his face flush. He grabbed the end of the winnower and pushed it away. "I would prefer that I knocked you off your polished boots for once, Mykah."

The other boy grinned. "Should I let you win? What good would that do you? Daman—when's your birthday?"

"Less than two weeks away."

"Practically tomorrow. And if your combat skills don't improve, your sixteen-year old butt will be—"

"I know what will happen," he said, cutting Mykah off. He wiped blood and sweat from his face and, with effort, managed to push himself to his feet. "My parents remind me every day. I don't need to get it from you, too."

"I'm only trying to help. The more you practice, the less likely you are to . . ."

Panic? he thought, silently completing the sentence. Freeze? Die, or be sentenced to something even worse? "I know preparation is important."

"You need to change the way you think about the Winnowing. It's more than just a ceremony. It's life or death. It's the single event that decides everything."

"When my time comes to enter the Arena and face my opponent—"

"Not your opponent. Your *enemy*." Mykah frowned.

"Right. That's what I kept thinking as we fought. The enemy. But how can someone be my enemy when I have no reason to dislike them?"

"I know you don't like to fight, Daman."

"I can fight," he said, perhaps too quickly. "I just want something worth fighting for."

"You can't expect to understand everything about our world. The Sentinel moves in strange and mysterious ways."

"I don't want to talk about it right now. I should be home."

Together they walked toward their homes in the village. His leg ached from the combat, but he was not about to let that show. His face was caked with blood, but he brushed it off and acted as if nothing unusual had occurred.

Everything Mykah said was true, of course. And everything his parents said as well. If he proved victorious at the Winnowing, he would join Merrindale's elite. He might become an Administrator, one of those who ran the village and enforced the Sentinel's Laws and Ways. Perhaps he could even join the Black Sentry, as Mykah had done. At the least he would be given a respectable trade. But if he lost . . . well, he preferred not to even think about it.

He glanced at Mykah, still silently trudging beside him. He treated Mykah shabbily and he knew it. They had been friends for as long as he could remember—longer even. Mykah had always been stronger and braver. Mykah had faced the Winnowing two months ago like a hero. Now he wore the distinctive dark uniform and goggled headgear that identified him as one of Merrindale's most important citizens—a lawkeeper. He already had a fine house. Soon a wife would be assigned to him, then a slave. Perhaps several slaves, as his career progressed.

Mykah generously agreed to these daily practice sessions to improve his skills, to teach him a few tricks that might be useful at his Winnowing. But nothing Mykah tried or taught made any difference. Time after time, when he heard the commencement gong sound, his heart clutched and his feet froze and the combat was over before it began. Every time he fought, he lost. And if that happened again in two weeks, his life would be finished. He was so worried about it he could think about little else. He tried as hard as he could. He was strong and smart and thought himself reasonably brave. But he never won.

He did not want to live a low, debased life, separated from everyone he ever knew or loved. He did not want to disappoint his parents. His fear that he would do both tore him apart. And it did not help that everyone kept reminding him just how close his Winnowing was.

They reached Mykah's home, a three-room thatched-roof cottage with real glass in the windows. He had it all to himself, at least for the moment. He waved goodbye and tried to choke back the thoughts coursing through his brain. He knew he shouldn't resent his best friend—but he did.

He left Mykah's neighborhood and entered his own, where the houses were smaller, regardless of how many people lived in them, the windows were boarded over with wooden planks, and the roofs leaked during the rainy season.

Since he was a small boy, he had counted the houses on his street. It had helped him find his own home—since all the houses looked alike. Each house followed the same pattern and was built in precisely the same way. To a small boy, it could be confusing. Now he did it out of habit.

A few moments later, he arrived at his home. He opened the front door quietly, hoping he could get to his room without attracting much attention.

Once again, his hopes were dashed.

He found both his mother and father standing just beyond the door waiting for him.

"Hello," his father said. His mother looked at him, her eyes like small stones.

"Hello," he returned, barely above a whisper.

"So . . ." He knew his father was trying to act casual, as if there was nothing in particular they wanted to know. But the effort was wasted. "Did you do anything of interest today?"

He tried to avoid the subject, even though he knew it was pointless. "Nothing much."

His father nodded. "But I notice your face is red and bruised."

"It's nothing."

"Every day this week you've come home bruised or battered in one way or another. Did you have another practice session with Mykah?"

"Yes."

He sensed his father already knew the answer to his next question. His mother, unfortunately, was not content with tacit communication.

"Don't you think we have a right to know what happened?" she asked.

"He beat me. That's what happened. He demolished me. Like always."

"Daman, this is important. Your whole—"

"Isn't it time for dinner, Martha?" his father said, cutting in.

She gave him a harsh glare, then acquiesced. "Past time. Wash up, then come to the table."

When he arrived at the dinner table, he took his traditional seat silently, hoping they could get through the meal without discussing the obvious subject. As soon as he was seated, Xander, their slave, served the food.

Xander was relatively new to their household. Father was the village baker, not an Administrator or one of the more prestigious tradesmen in the community. It had taken his father twenty years to accumulate enough Merit to have a slave assigned to him, and even then, all he got was a boy, one not much older than his son. By comparison, Mykah, as a member of the Black Sentry, would probably have enough Merit for an adult slave before the end of the year.

He sensed that his father didn't much care whether he had a slave, perhaps even preferred not to have one. His mother was just the opposite. She never ran out of tasks for Xander. She had assigned him virtually every household chore imaginable.

He tried not to look at Xander as he passed by. Like all members of the slave class, he bore the Deformity—a protruding purplish bulge over his left temple. The Sentinel had decreed that all those bearing the Deformity should be slaves. They lived apart and were never permitted to participate in any of the village's social events.

Xander served the meal.

He noticed that Xander had failed to give him a boiled potato. "Boy."

Xander stopped, then turned. He did not speak. Slaves were not permitted to speak, except in response to a direct question.

"My potato." He noticed his father giving him a strange

look. Xander moved hastily and deposited a potato on the plate. He hovered for just a moment, as if waiting to see if anything else would be required.

"Thank you, Xander," his father said. "I think that'll be all for now."

Xander shuffled off to his position at the end of the small dining room.

His mother barely waited a bite. "Daman, you know how much we worry about you."

"I'm doing everything I can." He did not mean to be insolent. The words just spewed out of him. He was so tired of it, all the pressure, all the guilt, the constant sense of his own inadequacy.

"Trying isn't good enough. The Winnowing will determine the course of your entire life."

"Do you think I don't know that?"

"If you win, you'll have everything—a good job, a good home. Merit."

"I know, Mother."

"But if you lose, you could be killed."

"I won't be killed."

"If you lose, you'll do work day after day for the rest of your life. You'll be stuck in a hole you'll never climb out of."

"What's wrong with menial work?" he said, intentionally not looking at his father. His mother covered her face with her hands. "Oh, Daman, don't say that. Not even in jest."

"Father is a baker. That's not so bad."

"Your father spent twenty years shoveling human waste out of the sewers before he was deemed to have enough Merit to be a baker. And baking hardly puts him at the highest level of village society."

"If I have to shovel, I'll shovel."

His father cleared his throat. "Son . . . there's more to it than that."

"If you lose," his mother said, "you'll be taken—blindfolded—to another village, where you'll remain for the rest of your life. We'll never see you again."

"You're not telling me anything I don't already know. I don't see why you have to keep hammering away at this every—"

"Because I'm your mother." She looked at him with wide and pleading eyes. "You're my only son. The only son I have and the only son I'll ever have. I only want the best for you. I want you to have more than—" She checked herself again. A moment later, she restarted. "There hasn't been a night I haven't thought—what if your father had prevailed at his Winnowing? Think where we might be now. A better job, more slaves. More—"

"Martha," his father said quietly, "perhaps this isn't the time."

"Then when?" she shot back. "In two weeks it will be too late."

"Surely we could talk about something else."

"Daman, I don't mean to make you unhappy. But this is so important."

His father cleared his throat, then made a quick jerk of his head toward the corner, where Xander stood at attention.

His mother fell silent. The Sentinel frowned on displays of strong emotion. They were potentially harmful, disorderly. And she wouldn't want to start even the whisper of a rumor that she had disobeyed the Laws and Ways of the Sentinel.

"Please." Her voice was barely a whisper now. Her eyes watered. "Think about what we've said. If there's anything more you can do, anything at all—"

"I'll try, Mother," he said, fighting back tears of his own. "If there's anything I can do, I will. That's a promise." But even as he spoke the words, he had no idea what he could possibly do. His future was all but written. He would lose his Winnowing, and be exiled, and be condemned.

CHAPTER

# THREE

Daman rose early the next morning to help his father prepare his booth. The Spring Festival was the village's sole annual holiday and they wanted to be ready for it. Everyone in Merrindale congregated near the North Gate—the millers and bakers, the blacksmiths and wheelwrights, the parents and their children and, of course, the everpresent Black Sentry. All villages were assigned specialized duties, and Merrindale principally focused on food production, not only for itself but for several other villages. As a result, food figured prominently in the Festival. Market Square abounded with aromas and odors, all mouthwateringly appealing—and for a poor baker's son, torturously unobtainable.

His father and the other merchants set up carts or booths to display their wares. His father had black bread and spice cakes and a few simple pastries. The Sentinel frowned on frivolity in all matters, including food, but his father still managed to have a few treats for the village's children. Toddlers pressed against the booth, pointing, salivating. Even if they were not tall enough to see what was on display, their noses gave them a complete description. Many a parent eventually parted with one of his hard-won coins so his child could have something special for Festival Day.

On one occasion, about mid-morning, he watched a small boy whose parents could not afford treats depart looking dejected and disappointed. His father quietly crept behind the child and placed a small tart in his tiny hands. The elated expression transformed the boy's face.

"That is no way to run a business, husband," his mother said later.

His father smiled, then squeezed her hand. No matter what his mother said, his father would never change.

Around midday he first heard the rumor. Two children, much younger than he, standing some distance from his father's booth, exchanged some astonishing news.

"Is it true?" the small girl gasped, her eyes wide and incredulous.

"It must be," the boy replied. "Papa said the Magistrate told him."

"The Acolyte! Here?"

His heart raced. The Acolyte. The chief representative of the Sentinel in this district. The Acolyte had not appeared in Merrindale since before he was born.

At the close of every Festival, the villagers gathered in the Arena for the Celebration of the Sentinel. But a Celebration presided over by the Acolyte would be an extraordinary event. For poor Merrindale, it would be an honor of the highest magnitude.

"Don't become too excited, Daman," his father warned.

"But the Acolyte—!"

His father laid his hand upon his shoulder. "I don't want you to be disappointed, son. Our village is one of many. Barely a speck in the Sentinel's great empire. He's hardly likely to send his personal representative to our little celebration."

He returned to his work, but he didn't abandon hope that the children's whisperings would prove true.

He loved the Spring Festival. Although everyone was careful not to violate any of the Sentinel's prohibitions against frivolous behavior or deviant activities, the people of Merrindale tried to make the most of the Festival. Many of the small cottages were festooned with flags and drapes and other approved decorations. Many people wore bright hand-sewn costumes. Often a single color or pattern was worn by every member of a family. Eating and drinking and playing livened the festival, although the Black Sentry ensured that none of it reached a level that would be inappropriate for an event that was, after all, a celebration of the Sentinel. The Sentry patrolled the grounds in dark uniforms that covered their entire bodies and made them seem invulnerable. As the light dimmed, their goggles seemed to glow, an eerie orange. No one knew how it was done. No one but the Sentinel, of course.

He sat in his father's booth and inhaled deeply, drawing in the smell of farm animals brought for show and slaughter, the smoke from the blacksmith's fire, the dust kicked up by a hundred footfalls on the dirt roads lacing the village. He heard small children playing Creeper tag, the chirping of invisible birds, the creaking of cart wheels. He admired the perfectly spaced trees, each one equidistant from the other, precisely the same size and shape, framed by the twelve-foot-high fence that surrounded and protected the village. Everything was exactly as it had always been, as it should be, in the Sentinel's perfectly ordered paradise. So he had been taught, even before he was old enough to understand.

As the Festival Day progressed, many familiar faces passed his father's booth—friends and families he had known his entire life. They greeted Citizen Bodie, the Systems Administrator, and his passel of six children, all of whom appeared to be systematically tormenting one another. Since Bodie won his Winnowing years before, he had achieved enough Merit to be permitted this almost unprecedented number of children. Of all the senior members of the Administration, Bodie was the friendliest. Of course, he had good reason to be merry.

On the other hand, poor Mister Cantrell, the village blacksmith for more than forty years, still had not Merited children or even a wife. In a few years, it would be his time to retire to Balaveria, never having known the blessings of family.

And there was Mister Blackthorne, the physic who, although he had achieved sufficient Merit some time before, still had no children. If there was no change soon, his wife would be reassigned, in accordance with the Laws and Ways of the Sentinel.

He also spotted the Garrett family, including their daughter, Brita, who was only a month older than he was. She would soon be assigned a husband. A popular rumor held that she would be assigned to Mykah. Even though Mykah was his friend, this prospect bothered him—more than he would ever have admitted. Brita was a strange, proud girl—and she had fascinated him since they were small children. She was the only girl in the village with yellow hair. Even her mother did not have it. She talked fast and often used words he did not understand.

"Greetings, Daman," Brita said, as she paused at his father's booth.

"Uh . . . hello. Greetings." He dared a look at her, and saw that she was not entirely her usual self. Her face seemed drawn and tired. "Are you well?"

"I'm magnificent," she said. "Only exhausted. I didn't sleep well last night."

He struggled for words. "It . . . is warm at night this time of year."

"That's utterly irrelevant." She looked mildly annoyed. "I've been having dreams. Strange dreams."

"About the festival?"

She looked as if she thought him utterly hopeless. "No, not about the Festival. Or Merrindale. About other places, other people."

"But—how can that be?" He knew Brita had never been beyond the fence surrounding Merrindale. Only those in the Administration were allowed to travel, and then only in accordance with strict, regimented plans pre-approved by the Sentinel. Those who lost their Winnowing would only travel once, when they were taken from their families and transported to another village. And they would be blindfolded for the entire journey—for their own safety. They would see nothing.

"It was just a dream," Brita said quickly. "Are you ready for your Winnowing?"

"Of course. Have you . . . been assigned?"

"Not yet." A strange expression crossed her face.

"Do you have any . . . preferences?"

"Would it make any difference if I did? Don't be so stupid, Daman. The Magistrate will do the will of the Sentinel, and the Sentinel will do whatever he wants, and there's not a thing any of us can do about it." She turned away from the booth and rejoined her parents.

Her words lingered even after she left. He had often thought the same—but he had never heard anyone express such thoughts out loud.

A Black Sentry platoon passed by. Although in uniform, they were apparently off-duty, because they did not march in formation, two had removed their masks, and one was accompanied by a slave. The Sentry typically did not permit slaves to accompany them when they performed official duties because it was thought slaves should not be trusted.

He knew the slave, a short, broad-shouldered man called Martin. He served as pack animal for the entire group, toting their food and drink. One Sentry snapped his fingers, and Martin immediately pressed a flask to his lips. Another did the same. Because Martin was slow to respond, the Sentry cuffed the slave soundly on the side of his face.

He turned away. He did not like seeing people mistreated, even if they were slaves. Bad enough to have so little personal freedom without being publicly humiliated.

An older man approached his father's booth—Mister Hayes, one of the elders of the village. He kept animals for slaughter near the North Gate. A patch of gray highlighted each side of his head. In a few years he would turn fifty, retire, and travel to Balaveria—a paradise where those who obeyed the Laws and Ways would live forever at the right hand of the Sentinel.

As usual, Mister Hayes came not to trade but to talk. "Have you heard the news, Mister Adkins?"

"I've heard the gossip," his father replied.

"What do you think about it?"

"I hear rumors about the coming of the Acolyte every year at this time. But he never comes."

Hayes frowned. "I'm not talking about that foolishness. I'm talking about Mister Blackthorne."

His father's eyes darkened. "What about him?"

"The Prosecutor has ruled. He is to lose his wife, and probably his livelihood."

"I am—sorry to hear that," His father said haltingly.

Hayes shrugged. "He knows the Laws and Ways, as we all do. He failed to produce a child. We have too few women of childbearing age. We cannot allow them to be wasted."

His father nodded but remained silent. He knew his father

was prudent and he should do the same. But he could not keep his mouth closed. "This hardly seems fair. They've been married for almost ten years and have always been happy. He's the best physic in Merrindale."

"He knows the Laws and Ways," Hayes intoned.

"But surely it's not his fault that he has no children." Although he was hardly an expert, he knew enough of such things to believe that this was true.

Hayes' eyes rose to meet Daman's father. "Mister Adkins, your son does not appear to be well versed in the Laws and Ways of the Sentinel."

His father flushed. "Oh—I'm sure Daman did not mean—"

"Then what did he mean?"

"He meant nothing. He's just a boy. Not even of Winnowing age. He knows nothing of these matters."

"He should be better instructed in the Laws and Ways. Someone might be tempted to report him to the Black Sentry as a blasphemer." Mister Hayes lowered his eyes. "Are you a blasphemer, son?"

He did not meet Hayes's gaze. "No, sir. I'm not."

"I'm glad to hear it." Hayes talked a bit longer about nothing at all, then finally left. He was relieved—but he could see that his father was even more relieved. His mother left abruptly, saying she needed to retrieve something from their home.

Some time later, Xander delivered a fresh batch of supplies. As always, Daman tried not to look at him. He didn't know why. Xander just made him uncomfortable.

"Thank you, Xander," his father said. "Is everything well at the bakery?"

Xander nodded courteously, then set his bundle down on a bench. He was a strong boy, with broad shoulders and tough sinewy arms. A lifetime of servitude undoubtedly produced firm muscles.

"Any news of the day?"

Xander hesitated. Like all slaves, he was cautious about speaking. In this instance, though, he had been asked a direct question.

"Have you heard the news?" Xander asked.

"What news would that be?" his father asked.

Xander's voice dropped to a whisper. "The Acolyte. They say he is coming to our village. That he will preside over the Celebration."

"What business would the Sentinel's chief representative have here?"

"I don't know, but they say he's coming all the same." Xander stopped speaking, perhaps afraid he had said too much. His eyes drifted toward a plate of freshly baked spice cakes. Xander was a large boy—nearly twice his weight and half a head taller. He probably had an outsized appetite as well.

His father smiled. "You must be starved, Xander. Please take one of those cakes. Maybe two. Here, I'll—"

His father stopped. His mother had reentered the booth, and the expression on her face was set and serious.

"I'm sorry, Xander," she said, blocking his access to the cakes. "I believe you're needed back at the bakery."

Xander looked as if he'd been pierced through the heart. "But—"

"That was an instruction, not a question."

Xander fell silent.

"Go."

Xander turned away, crestfallen, and left the booth.

His parents stepped outside and had a private conversation. He couldn't hear what they were saying, but the tone of the discussion was agitated.

A few moments later, his father returned to the booth, lips pursed. He did not say a word. He took two slices of the spice cakes and pressed them into his son's hands. "Go find him."

He needed no further explanation. He bolted out of the booth and ran down the dusty crossroads, searching through the thick of the festival traffic for their slave. Celebration time neared, and people packed the roads.

"Daman, have you heard the news?"

Mykah shouted at him from the side of the road. He hadn't seen his friend since the humiliating practice session the day before. Mykah had always been stronger and more popular, even when they were small boys. He suspected that many people in the village were amazed they were friends. But there was a secret reason for their long-standing friendship.

Once, when they were eight and played together near Blaine River, Mykah slipped on ice and fell in. At that time, he could not swim, but Daman could, due to his father's great love of the sport. He managed to pull Mykah from the paralyzing water. Not only did he save Mykah's life—he didn't tell anyone about it afterward. Ever since, Mykah had been his loyal companion.

"Have you heard?" Mykah asked.

"I do not believe the Acolyte would have any reason to—"

"What has the Acolyte got to do with anything?"

He stopped. "What are you talking about then?"

"This news is about me." He pressed his thumb to his chest. "I've been accepted for the Black Sentry's Rover team."

He stared back at his friend, not knowing what to say.

"Is that not incredible news?"

"But—you're only sixteen—"

"They've made an exception for me." He beamed. "Isn't that incredible?"

He hesitated, not wanting to reveal his feelings, which he

did not fully understand himself. He should be pleased for his friend, but somehow, the thought of him becoming even more involved with the Sentry made him feel cold and distant. Plus, if Mykah joined the Rover team, he would be permitted to travel throughout the Sentinel's lands. He would see the world beyond the tall fence. "But it's so soon—"

"Why should I wait? An opportunity like this won't come often. I can make a valuable contribution to the Sentry."

Even in his short lifetime, he had seen families torn apart by the Black Sentry—mothers taken from their families and reassigned, runaways hunted down and dragged back to their village, good men destroyed or exiled for violating the Laws and Ways, fathers forced to perform hated occupations.

Mykah continued. "I want to be a part of the Sentry's great work. To serve the Sentinel in all his glory. To see the world. Haven't you ever wanted to know what lies beyond this village?"

Mykah's words stung. He knew the hard red earth of the village, the flat yellow plains of the Nether End, the green groves that lined Blaine River near the Forest of the Creepers. But he knew nothing of the world beyond. And chances were, he never would.

"I want a life of excitement," Mykah said. "A life of adventure. I don't want to spend all my days in this dusty village slaughtering pigs and baking—" He stopped short. "I'm not saying that sort of life is bad. For some people, it may be perfect. But not for me."

"Of course not."

"I want to do the Sentinel's will. After all, the Sentinel's will is all."

"Yes," he echoed, "the Sentinel's will is all."

"Won't you congratulate me, Daman?"

He pressed his hand against his friend's shoulder. "Yes. Congratulations. I'm happy for you."

Mykah stared the other way, toward the North Gate. His jaw slackened.

"What is it?"

Mykah's hand rose, first to point, then to block the reflected light from his eyes. "The Acolyte," he said, his voice barely more than a whisper. "He's here."

# FOUR

Daman watched as the Procession of the Acolyte strode through the North Gate and entered the crossroads of the village in shimmering splendor. The light of the midday sun reflected off the sea of white robes, momentarily blinding all onlookers. Five attendants walked on either side of the Acolyte, who wore a simple robe with the gold braid that designated him as one of the Sentinel's chosen. He wore a tall peaked hat upon his head, predominantly white but fringed with lines of purple. A Black Sentry contingent circled around the Procession.

The Acolyte waved to the dumbstruck spectators as he passed by, smiling and making the gesture of blessing. People fell to their knees, faces buried in the dirt.

The merchants closed their booths. Families gathered, and although no formal instruction was given, all fell in line behind the Procession.

He found his parents and followed with the others. No words were spoken, not even whispers. Everyone seemed spellbound, caught up in the magnitude of the moment.

At last they arrived at the public entrance to the Arena. The

Procession moved to the center, while the villagers scrambled for seats in the gallery. A large object, almost the size of a shed, rested near the place where the Procession stopped. A large canvas covered it so no one could tell what it was.

When at last they found their seats, the Acolyte stepped out from the ring of attendants, faced the gathered throng, and lifted his hands high into the air.

He spoke in a clear, booming voice. "The Sentinel is our heart, our soul, and our salvation."

The congregation repeated his words in unison. "The Sentinel is our heart, our soul, and our salvation."

The Acolyte continued. "The Sentinel protects us from evil, and the evil in our own hearts."

"The Sentinel protects us from evil," the people of Merrindale chanted back, "and the evil in our own hearts."

"May the Sentinel be with you, always."

"And also with you."

The Acolyte made the sign of blessing and finished the lengthy litany all those present knew well.

As Daman gazed about the Arena, he saw many tears. This surprise visit from the Sentinel's own representative moved some of the villagers more than words could express.

But his heart was strangely unaffected.

After they completed the appropriate litany for the Spring Festival, the Acolyte lowered his arms and gazed out toward the assemblage with a warm, soothing smile. "Children of the Sentinel, thank you for joining me today to celebrate the rich and fertile bounty of our patient Master."

"Long live the Sentinel!" someone shouted. A tumult of cheering and applause followed.

The Acolyte's smile broadened. "It pleases me to see that the Sentinel is loved here. I wish everyone felt as you do." A trace of darkness crept into his voice. "Alas, it is not so. Unbelievable though it may seem, there are those who rebel against the Sentinel, who struggle with their patient Master. They resist his Laws and his Ways. Many of these foolish Rebels have banded together to restore the malevolent weapons of the past and use them against the Sentinel and his people."

"No!" a woman shrieked from the stands. Several more cries followed.

"Your anger is understandable, but it is not the way of the Sentinel. We must live in peace—and order—as we always have done. But be aware that Rebels are amongst you even as we speak. Dangerous exiles have been spotted outside the gate to this very village, men hunted for heinous crimes.

"There is one man in particular," he continued, "a very old, very foolish man, who has taken something that belongs to the Sentinel, something he hopes to use for his own savage purposes. If you see this man, you must report it immediately to the Black Sentry, so that order may be preserved and justice may prevail.

"Remember," the Acolyte said, raising a finger, "this old man is crafty. He is the Great Deceiver. He and his imps will try to fool you. You must not listen. You must remain true to the Sentinel. He has always cared for you. He is our only hope for survival."

The Acolyte laid a hand upon the huge draped object. "You must never forget that we live in a hostile, evil world. The Creepers swarm just beyond the fence, flinging their tentacles at all who come within their grasp. The Savages infest the untamed forests, perpetuating their unspeakable barbaric acts. At one time, the Constructs, the sworn enemies of Man, thrived everywhere. They dominated us and controlled our every movement. The Sentinel vanquished these demons and restored the world to order. But do not be fooled, brave Children of the Sentinel. Those enemies are only dormant, not dead. They could rise again. They lie in wait for their opportunity."

He grabbed the canvas with both hands. "Peer into the face of evil." With one sweeping gesture, he jerked the canvas off the huge hidden object.

The crowd gasped as if their breath had been stolen from their lungs. All eyes were fixed on the horrible . . . *monstrosity* . . . in the center of the Arena.

This huge hard object was unlike anything Daman had ever seen before, unnatural in design and clearly malicious in purpose. Most of it was green, though partly yellow, with two large wheels on either side and smaller wheels in front. A rectangular cab rested at the top, and through transparent glass he saw a chair such as a man might sit upon. In front of all this, low to the ground, an array of glistening curved blades hung like the teeth of this ravenous beast.

Children cowered, covering their eyes. Many adults did the same.

"Behold the Construct!" the Acolyte cried. "These hateful creatures once ruled the earth. They chased Man and herded him like beasts. Only the Sentinel saved us from their evil dominion. And only he prevents their return."

More squeals flew from the gallery. The thought of that hideous Construct advancing toward them, carving humans with its cruel blades, sent shivers down his spine.

With the help of two attendants, the Acolyte replaced the canvas, masking the green and yellow abomination.

"Today, thanks to the Sentinel, we are free," the Acolyte continued. "Free to live noble, orderly lives, fulfilling the works of the Sentinel, furthering his great Laws and Ways. Children of the Sentinel, do not provide safe harbor to those who let these evil beings dominate us. The Constructs have been vanquished, banished, and forbidden, and they must remain thus always. So saith the Sentinel."

"So saith the Sentinel," the crowd chanted in response.

"Keep the faith, my blessed people. May the Sentinel be with you, always."

"And also with you."

Questions riddled Daman's brain. Evil or not, he wanted to know more about the Construct in the center of the Arena. What was it, exactly? What did it do? It did not appear to have a life of its own. Why would it chase or herd people? Was it some sort of weapon? A tool? If it were an enemy to men, why did it have a seat for one?

He knew these were vile questions. He had been taught all his life that people were better off knowing as little as possible about the Ancients. All they needed to know was that it was a time of horror and that the Sentinel had saved them from it. His curiosity should end there.

But it did not.

What's wrong with me? he wondered, as he gazed at the enraptured faces around him. Do I have some sort of deviant, twisted personality? Why don't I worship and adore the Sentinel like the others do?

Or was it simply the fear of the Winnowing that perverted his thoughts?

"Enough," the Acolyte pronounced. "This is a Celebration. So let us celebrate. Bring forth the Combatants."

The attendants parted to make way for two young men from the village. He knew them both. One was called Victor. His father had a small mill near the river. The other was Evan, whose father kept sheep and other feedstock. He had known Evan all his life. He, Mykah, and Evan had often spent summer nights swapping stories about the Creepers.

The Acolyte stepped between the boys and laid a hand on

each shoulder. "It is the right and duty of these two boys, the two oldest in the village who have not yet achieved the age of Winnowing, to enter into combat on this day. In this manner, the Sentinel's will shall be done."

The Acolyte guided the two boys to the large octagonal grid with intersecting areas of red and yellow.

"Victor, you shall fight upon the red." He placed Victor in the appropriate starting area. "And you, Evan, shall play on the yellow." He moved Evan to the opposite side of the grid. "Bring forth the winnowers."

The Acolyte weighed each winnower in his hand, ensuring that they were of equal heft and strength. Then he handed one to each boy. He stepped out of the grid and once again raised his hands into the air.

"Just as the Sentinel once fought for you, so you now shall fight for the right to carry on his great plan, to ensure that his work is never forgotten. You are our future. Let no man forget the importance of what is done in this blessed Arena.

"When I give the signal," he continued, "the Winnowing shall begin. When I drop my hands, the gong will sound and you will fight—to the finish."

# FIVE

Daman heard the gong sound and the Winnowing commenced. The people in the gallery shouted and cheered, some for a particular champion, some simply caught up in anticipation of the bloodshed that would follow.

Victor and Evan circled each other within the octagonal grid, each keeping a careful watch on his feet, making sure he did not blunder into his opponent's territory. This was the Patience Gambit, where the combatant played a cautious opening, biding his time, hoping the mounting pressure would impel his enemy to make an unwise attack.

Victor and Evan were both strong fighters. The Patience Gambit went on for almost five minutes, the tension mounting with each cycle around the multi-colored grid.

Victor made a sudden change of direction, from clockwise to counterclockwise, catching Evan off-guard. He lost his balance and nearly stepped onto the red. The crowd drew in its breath, gasping at the near miss.

Evan appeared to tire. He held his stick lower.

*Come on*, Evan. Daman knew his friend could stand watch over the flocks for hours. But a day in the fields was probably the equivalent of ten seconds in this Arena.

Victor rushed toward Evan, swinging hard with the bulb end of his winnower. Evan faltered. The winnower clubbed him on the back of his head. He hooked Victor's winnower with the blade end of his own. The two sticks were interlocked, one wrapped around the other. The boys engaged in a fearsome tug-of-war, each pulling with all his might to yank his opponent onto the other color.

The crowd roared. Victor appeared to have the advantage. Evan staggered, reeling from the blow to his head.

Daman found himself thinking of Evan's parents, both kind and friendly people, and what it would mean to them if Evan lost.

And then, without warning, the balance shifted. Evan dropped to the ground, as if his legs disappeared. Victor was unprepared for the sudden move. He lost his equilibrium and teetered, just long enough for Evan to jab his stick between Victor's legs and twist, throwing his opponent even further off balance. Victor tumbled precipitously forward.

His right foot hovered over the yellow.

The shouting from the gallery reached a fevered pitch. Even those who lacked any personal involvement with the players shouted and cheered. At the last possible moment, Victor flung himself back onto his own color, but as he did so, Evan whirled and caught Victor with the sharp end of his winnower. The blade cut into Victor's side, just below the ribs. Victor cried out. Blood splashed down on the grid.

The tumult from the stands reached a thunderous high.

Victor struggled to his feet, one hand clutching the gaping wound. He seemed wobbly, uncertain. He knew what they all knew.

The Winnowing would not last much longer now.

Victor, both hands on his stick despite his wound, bravely blocked and parried his enemy's blows. Each thrust knocked him lower. His resistance weakened.

Evan landed another blow to the bleeding gut, and Victor tumbled to the ground. A cry rang out from the gallery. The crowd leaned forward, anticipating the final moment.

Evan raised the bladed end of his winnower and ran at Victor for a final lunge. A second before he connected, Victor rolled out of the way.

He had not been as exhausted as he led his opponent to believe.

Evan's stick rammed into the ground where Victor had been with such force that Evan was completely thrown off kilter. He tottered, twisted sideways, did everything possible to hold his position.

But nothing worked. He fell forward, his left foot touching down on the red.

The penalty gong sounded.

For one turn of the glass, while Evan remained limited to the yellow, Victor attacked from all directions. With newfound energy, and despite his seeping wound, Victor came at Evan from every position at once, poking and prodding and piercing him in more than a half dozen places. Finally, Victor feinted with the pointed end of the winnower, then whirled around with the bulb end, smashing Evan in the face.

Evan fell, his body a blanket on the multi-colored Arena floor.

In the stands, Daman clenched his hands, his heart in a knot. This was not right. This was simply not right . . .

Victor placed the sharp point of the winnower on Evan's chest, then raised his hands in triumph.

The Acolyte signaled the end of the Winnowing. "Congratulations, Victor Timmons. A lifetime of glorious service, doing the Sentinel's most important work, lies before you.

"Evan Martel," the Acolyte continued, "you have been winnowed. You know the choice that lies before you. Do you choose death or transportation?"

Evan hesitated so long observers wondered what he might say. "T—T—Transportation," he finally managed.

He would be taken by the Black Sentry—blindfolded—to another village, far from his friends and family. There he would be assigned some menial work or hard labor, which he would perform day after day until his eventual passage to Balaveria.

Victor, still dripping blood from the wound beneath his ribs, limped out of the Arena to cheers and applause.

The Acolyte was not finished. "There is one matter more. Sentence has been passed against a member of this village, a man called Joseph Anton. Step forth, Joseph Anton."

Several members of the Black Sentry dragged Mister Anton from the side of the Arena.

Daman's heart fell. He knew Mister Anton well, and he knew why he was being sentenced. He had a barn near Blaine River where he kept pigs. This year, however, the river over-flowed and flooded his barn. Most of his animals were killed.

"The Prosecutor has found this man guilty of failing to pay tribute to the Sentinel. We all must give our Master the first and best part of the bounty. But Joseph Anton did not. He hid his wealth and evaded his duty."

"If I had given all that the Sentinel demanded," Anton said, "my wife and daughters would have starved."

"The time of choosing is upon you, Joseph Anton," the Acolyte boomed. "The Laws and Ways of the Sentinel permit no exceptions. What will it be—exile or execution?"

As Daman knew too well, exile was even worse than transportation. It meant total separation from this or any village, living alone with no access to food or protection from the Creepers and the Savages. Most villagers considered exile a coward's way out, or a fool's. Death was a certainty either way. The only difference was that execution would be quick, while the death resulting from exile might be protracted and painful.

"Execution," Anton said.

But what would happen to Anton's children? They would be left without a provider. Their only hope was that his former wife would be assigned a new husband, but that seemed unlikely, since she was no longer of childbearing age.

Anton was led to the center of the Arena. A canvas drape was placed over his head. "This is the Shroud of the Sentinel," the Acolyte intoned. "From this day until the time of your execution, you are no longer a part of this community. You are no longer of the Sentinel."

How harsh that must be, Daman thought, to be irrevocably separated from everything you've ever known. Despite the fact that he had been told since birth of the wisdom of the Sentinel's Laws and Ways—it didn't seem right.

He hated the feelings swelling up in his heart—but he couldn't make them go away. This wasn't right. This simply wasn't right.

"So it is now and ever shall be for those who fail the Sentinel. The Laws and Ways are wise and must be obeyed."

The crowd repeated his words. "The Laws and Ways are wise and must be obeyed."

This litany continued for several minutes. Although he knew the words, he found he could not make himself repeat them. Glancing back over his shoulder, he saw the parents of Evan, the boy who had lost the Winnowing, slinking out of the Arena, their eyes streaked with tears. How could they endure the pain of knowing with absolute certainty that they would never see their son again?

He glanced to one side and noticed that, once again, his own father was looking at him.

"It is the Way of the Sentinel," his father said, without much feeling, answering the question he hadn't asked. "The Sentinel is a good and kind Master."

He didn't reply—because the thoughts boiling in his brain were too unformed to express. He had always admired his father, and he had always valued his opinion. But how could his father blindly accept what was so unjust? How could he respect someone who was willing to live with such inequity?

And what was happening to him. He did not remember even feeling this way about the Sentinel before. But now his anger all but overwhelmed him.

A moment later, Anton disappeared from sight. The cloak that had been placed atop him fluttered to the ground.

The Acolyte resumed his incantation. "Thus be delivered all those who have sinned against the Sentinel." He brought the Celebration to an end. "Remember all that I have told you. Remember the Laws and Ways of the Sentinel. Go now and live in harmony as the Sentinel has proscribed."

Daman left with his family, but he did not feel jubilant or festive. His stomach churned and his head throbbed. *What is wrong with me?* He felt as if something had snapped inside his brain. Or perhaps, a missing piece had fallen into place.

He remembered the word the Acolyte had used—Rebel. Was this what it was to be a Rebel? Was he thinking like the fiends who had terrorized the world of the Ancients with Constructs?

He knew almost nothing about such matters. But he knew what he had seen in the Arena today made his heart ache. He would miss Evan. How would his family replace him, both as a worker and as a son? How could there be any wisdom in the Laws and Ways if they resulted in such unnecessary hardship and cruelty?

And, he asked himself, if these Laws were wrong, how many of the other Laws governing the Sentinel's perfectly ordered paradise might be wrong?

# SIX

After the Celebration of the Sentinel concluded, Daman helped his father take down his booth. Then they returned to their small thatched-roof cottage.

Although there was much conversation at dinner, there was little discussion of what they witnessed in the Arena. His mother tried, alluding to Victor's clever triumph or "the unfortunate Mister Acton," but she was met by silence from both her husband and son.

After Xander cleared the table, his mother retired for the night.

"Daman," his father said, "I would like to speak with you."

He had no trouble guessing what the subject might be. His foolhardy outburst in front of Mister Hayes.

He stared down at the floor. "I'm sorry, Father. But when Mister Hayes talked so arrogantly, finding fault with poor Mister Blackthorne, a man who has never harmed anyone and has helped so many . . . I couldn't contain myself."

His father smiled slightly. "Mister Hayes is a blowhard. But what you did was foolish."

"Yes, sir. I know that."

"You do not want to become an enemy of the Black Sentry. They deal with their enemies in a ruthless and . . . orderly manner."

"Yes, Father. I know."

"I can see that something is troubling you. What is it?"

It would have been wiser to keep these thoughts inside, but he couldn't restrain himself. "It's so unfair, Father."

"What is?"

"Everything. Everything the Sentinel requires us to do. Forces us to do. Why can't people make their own decisions?"

"You know what you've been taught. There was a time when men were free to make their own decisions. Chaos reigned. The world was plagued by cruelty and inequity. Starvation and hardship. The Constructs dominated our lives." He paused. "The Sentinel saved us from all that. He gave us a safe, predictable way of life. A better way."

"I have heard that, yes." He mustered all his courage and looked directly into his father's eyes. "But I'm not sure I believe it. Do you believe it?"

"I believe . . ." His father stopped, then started again. "I believe there was another time. Before the Sentinel. Beyond that . . ." His voice faded.

"Please, Father. Tell me."

"Son, you have to understand. A parent has certain responsibilities. He can't do anything that might lead his child into a dangerous direction."

"Surely you see how cruel the Sentinel's Laws and Ways can be."

His father hesitated. "There was a time, perhaps, when I was much younger . . ." He shook his head fiercely, as if to erase the entire line of thought. His eyes darted toward a cupboard in which he kept pots and pans and other equipment, most of which had been handed down by the man who had been the village baker before him. "Let me show you something. I think you're old enough." He winked. "You can keep a secret, can't you?"

His father opened the cupboard, reached far into the back, and removed a small object that had previously been hidden.

It was round and smooth and attached to a rusted chain. Two gold arrows projected from the center of the face, which was covered with scratchings he did not understand.

"This," his father said proudly, "was created by the Ancients, the people who lived before the time of the Sentinel. It was called a Watch."

He took it gently into his hands. "What did it do?"

"By using the Watch, the Ancients were able to tell where they were in the day. Whether it was morning or evening. How much of the day had passed."

"But Father—we can tell those things simply by looking at the sky."

"Yes, I know, but with the Watch, you could tell *without* looking at the sky. Without even going outside. And with greater precision."

Was this an actual Construct? The evil creations he'd heard so much about for so long?

He examined it by the tarnished chain, wondering how it operated. Did the Ancients wear it around their necks? Did they lay it flat under the sun to catch a shadow? "Does it work?"

"No, it doesn't, I mean—its been so long, I—I don't—I—" He frowned. "To be honest, son, I don't really know."

"How could this tiny bauble tell them where they were in the day?"

He snatched it back. "Well, I don't know. But it could."

"How did you get it?"

"I had it from my father, who had it from his father. It's been passed down in this family for generations."

"If the Black Sentry knew—"

"Yes. Indeed." He returned it to its hiding place in the cupboard.

"And yet you keep it, Father."

He closed the cupboard. "I keep it because it represents time, and therefore reminds me that there was another time, when men were free to choose their own path."

"A time of chaos."

"Perhaps. Yet somehow, despite the chaos, they were able to create wondrous devices such as that one."

After they finished talking, they retired for the evening. But Daman did not sleep well. His rest was plagued by vivid dreams, dreams of a long-forgotten world in which men could tell the time without going outside, a world of Constructs with large vicious teeth, a world of danger and disharmony. A world of chaos.

A world he found himself longing for.

———

THE NEXT DAY, wherever Daman went, everyone talked about the Winnowing, Victor's triumph, and the surprise appearance of the Acolyte. He heard more and more about it until he was sick of the subject.

About midday, he passed near the Arena making a delivery of fresh baked bread for his father. He was winding his way through the curving dirt roads that interlaced the villagers' homes when a member of the Black Sentry—Benjamin Coffin— crossed his path. Coffin was in his forties. Early in his career he obtained an officer's commission on which he grew fat and indulgent. He rose to great importance in the village, second only to the Captain of the Guard.

Coffin rushed down the road accompanied by his personal slave, Fenton, who had been with him for many years. Apparently Coffin was too important to stop for a proper meal. Fenton tried to feed the gluttonous man as he walked, pushing bite-sized bits of beef into his mouth as they marched side-by-side.

Fenton stumbled and dropped one of the bites on the ground.

"Look what you've done, you clumsy oaf!" Coffin bellowed, grinding to a halt.

Fenton bent down and recovered the food, then brushed the dirt and sand from it.

Daman's stomach churned watching the poor slave grovel and scrape.

While Fenton was crouched down, Coffin withdrew his crop and cracked Fenton on the backside.

Fenton leaped into the air, wailing.

Coffin laughed. "Let that be a lesson to you, slave. Don't let it happen again. Understand?"

"Yes, Master," Fenton answered, his voice cracking. "I am sorry for my clumsiness. Please do not hurt me."

Coffin did not listen. He brought his crop around and hit the poor man again, this time on the side of his neck, not far from the purplish protuberance that distinguished the slave class. Fenton fell to his knees, crying in pain.

Daman turned away, unable to watch the pathetic spectacle any longer. Apparently it was not enough that men should have slaves to fulfill their every whim. They must mistreat them as well. How could this arrogant bully treat others with such contempt?

And then, he wondered, had his own treatment of Xander been any better?

He heard Coffin's crop crack again, he heard Fenton cry out, and before he knew what was happening, he saw a brown blur rush past him, intervening between the crop and the slave. Several moments passed before his eyes focused.

It was Xander. What did he think he was doing?

Xander positioned himself between Coffin and Fenton. He grabbed Coffin's arm and held it fast, preventing him from beating his slave again. They stood face-to-face, glaring into one another's eyes.

"What do you think you're doing?" Coffin spat out.

Now that he'd been spoken to, Xander had the right to reply. "I'm sure you did not intend to act so cruelly, Lieutenant Coffin. Obviously the heat of the day has inflamed your temper."

"Get away from me!" Coffin tried unsuccessfully to shrug Xander off. His already florid face flushed. His considerable belly vibrated.

Xander held his ground. "I cannot let you beat this man like a rug in public. He has done nothing to merit such treatment."

He could not believe what he heard. For a slave to speak in such a manner was forbidden. To speak in such a manner to a Black Sentry lieutenant was suicide. And yet, he couldn't help but admire the enormous strength Xander displayed. Despite his low station in life, Xander found the courage to do what no one else would.

Coffin's eyes focused on Xander's bulging temple. "You're a slave! And you dare—!" His eyes widened and his jowls shook. "I am ordering you to step aside."

Xander did not budge. "I am respectfully declining to obey."

Coffin's temper boiled so hot he thought the top of the man's head might blow off. The heavy man lacked the strength to get past Xander. When he realized it was hopeless, he stepped back and lowered his crop.

"The Captain of the Guard will hear about this," Coffin said, eyes ablaze.

"Of that I have no doubt," Xander quietly replied.

Coffin stormed away, heading for the local Sentry headquarters not far from the Arena. A few moments later, Fenton scampered off behind him, obviously unsure where to go or what to do next.

He suddenly realized they had become the focus of a great deal of attention. Several dozen passersby had stopped to observe the spectacle. Frowning, he ducked into a nearby alleyway. He wanted to speak to Xander alone, but he lost the slave somewhere in the darkness.

Someone was following him. He walked faster, then faster still, then ran. Until the alleyway came to a dead end.

Trapped, he turned to confront his pursuer.

To his surprise, he saw it was not the Black Sentry, but Brita. "That...was a good thing you did," she said quietly.

What" He was confused. Then he realized Xander hid behind a nearby pile of crates.

The slave emerged. "I accomplished very little."

"I disagree. I think you acted heroically."

Did she really think so? He gazed at her amazing blonde tresses.

"You saved poor Fenton from a beating," Brita continued.

"He will have twice that beating tonight when he returns to his master's home," Xander rejoined. "And there is nowhere else he can go. I should not have intervened. My temper got the best of me." He pressed one fist against the flat of his hand. "I could not stand idly by while that pompous—" He did not finish his sentence.

Daman had never heard Xander speak so many words at once, much less with such passion.

"Still," Brita said, "if others follow your example—"

"Who will follow? I will be transported as soon as this event is reported."

"We will not ship you anywhere, Xander," he said. "You will not be punished."

"You will have no choice, once the Captain of the Guard reports this to the Magistrate."

He fell silent. He knew Xander was correct. Coffin would never let this end without seeking redress.

"I will speak to my father. We'll do everything we can to see that you aren't punished."

"Yes, I'm sure the village baker will have the clout to rewrite the Laws and Ways."

He bit down on his bottom lip. He knew they both spoke from frustration. "He can try."

"And why would you do that?"

"Because . . . until just now . . . I thought I was the only one in the village who . . . questioned the way we live. The way we are forced to live."

"You were wrong," Brita said, without explaining. "But Daman, how can we change—"

"There will be no change so long as people are not free to express their own thoughts. As long as we are controlled by a power we cannot even see."

Brita stiffened. He couldn't understand why. Then he detected movement in the shadows behind her. Someone was back there, staying at a distance. Listening. Lurking.

He barely caught a glimpse of the top of a head, but he still felt certain he could identify it. Mister Hayes. The man who had accused him of blasphemy.

Brita cleared her throat. "I think perhaps the heat has begun to affect your mind, Daman."

"Yes," he said, catching on. "Perhaps it has. I'm babbling nonsense."

"You don't know what you were saying. Xander, help your master back home. A cool drink will do wonders for him."

He caught a glimpse of Mister Hayes scurrying away. Had they fooled him? Or was he on his way to report what he heard to the Captain of the Guard?

If he didn't learn to control his tongue, he would soon find himself confronted with the same choice as poor Mister Anton.

Exile or execution. If they gave him any choice at all.

———

Daman found a drink at Market Square. Xander left to perform his daily duties. Brita said she had chores to finish before sundown. He doubted it. More likely she didn't want to be associated with this heretic, this crazed madman who blasphemed the Sentinel. When the Black Sentry came for him, she didn't want to be anywhere near.

At the end of the day, his father sent him to the Nether End of the village to make deliveries to the slave quarters. He hated these jobs more than any other. Although it was still within the protective fence surrounding the village, the Nether End was the farthest point from where Daman and his friends lived. The Nether End was populated by slaves dwelling in shabby, filth-ridden housing. He could sympathize with the hard life they led, but the thought of being surrounded by all those deformed people, shuffling back and forth with their malformed heads, gave him shivers.

He had made many deliveries here over the years, and it was not more than a mile from the forested banks of Blaine River, where he and Mykah and Evan had often played as boys—and where he had once saved Mykah's life.

After making his deliveries, he decided to take the long route home, following the tall fence. At one point, he heard an unsettling hissing, rattling noise just beyond the fence. Like the slithering of wet leaves.

Could that be a Creeper? The men of the village said the Creepers lurked just outside the fence, eternally searching for a way in. Like most in the village, he had never actually seen a Creeper, but he had been told that they were deadly, that they could kill with a single blow, and that no one had ever managed to kill one.

He plunged back into the forest, with its perfectly spaced and identical trees, taking a diagonal route toward home. He knew a shallow place where the river could be crossed. Since he had completed his chores for the day, he took his time, mulling over everything that had happened. Before long, he had wandered farther south than he had intended.

He remained deep in reverie until suddenly he heard footsteps behind him, footsteps approaching rapidly.

"Help me," a hoarse voice gasped. "Please help me."

Rising up the crest of a hill, he saw a man like none he had seen before in his entire life. His face was strange. Deformed. His skin folded in on itself, rippling down the face and sagging under the chin. Even though he had never seen anything like it, he understood what it must be.

This man was old. Older than anyone he had ever seen. Far older.

The man's hair and beard were white as clouds. His back was hunched, but he was still able to move at a steady pace. His dress seemed familiar yet strange. He wore his collar backwards, so that the white rounded part showed through the opening at the top of his tunic. He carried a small backpack.

A sudden thought struck Daman. Was this the man the Acolyte had mentioned? The Rebel who fought against the Sentinel himself?

"Please," the Old Man repeated. "I need your help."

He did not need to ask why. He could see for himself. Down the path at the foot of the hill he spotted the Old Man's pursuers. They were too far away to distinguish their faces, but he could make out their black shirts with shiny gold buttons, their goggled masks bearing the Emblems of Authority, their whip-like crops strapped to the hip.

The Black Sentry.

# SEVEN

Daman couldn't decide what to do next. Could the Sentry identify him from this distance? Could he and the Old Man possibly escape?

"Quickly!" the Old Man urged. "Help me."

There was no time to think, no time to debate. There was only time to act, to do what seemed right.

He took the Old Man's hand and led him down the far side of the hill. They had to leave the main road or they had no chance of eluding the Sentry. Fortunately, he knew this area well. He was pleased to find that the Old Man, despite his age and obvious fatigue, could still move quickly.

The far side of the hill was thicker with trees. He reasoned that the trees would provide cover as they made their descent. They raced down the hill, zigzagging past the round boulders and rectangular hedges.

Still, as they approached the bottom of the hill, the Black Sentry were not far behind.

He started down the trail that would pass through the densest part of the forest. He could hear the Old Man gasping and wheezing beside him. Occasionally his feet would tangle or he would trip over an obstacle, but he never stopped for long.

"Only about a fourth of a mile further," he said, not breaking his pace. "Then we'll reach the Collins place. There are haystacks and barns and other hiding places. We'll be much safer there than out in the open."

The Old Man nodded, without slowing. His face was sunbaked and his eyes seemed large and watery. He moved without complaint, but he could not possibly keep up this pace indefinitely.

They rounded a corner and, in the distance, he spotted the Collins barn. A moment later, further down the road, he saw something else. Six dark spots dotting the road.

Another Black Sentry platoon.

They froze. The Sentry were both before them and behind them. There was nowhere to go.

He felt a heavy sickness in his stomach. He had acted impulsively—and stupidly. All he'd wanted to do was help this man —and now perhaps his rash actions had doomed them both.

"I'm sorry. I've failed you."

"Not yet," the Old Man said, pulling him toward the fence. "We must cross into the forest."

"But the Creepers—"

"—can't be worse than the Black Sentry."

"How will you get over the fence?"

"The same way I came in."

"But—" He heard the black boots drawing closer. Soon the Sentry would be near enough to identify him. A few seconds after that, they would be captured. And he knew what the penalty would be for assisting a Rebel. The Acolyte had made that abundantly clear.

"There is no place to plant your feet. How can we climb the fence?"

"Just watch." To his surprise, the Old Man reached into his backpack and pulled out a rope with a metal hook on the end. He swung the hook in the air a few times, then hurled it toward the top of the fence. The hook clamped down on the top snugly.

The Old Man pulled on the rope a few times, tightening it. He stepped back several paces, then made a run at it. He leapt up, and hoisted himself to the top, walking sideways up the fence. Despite the huge difference between their ages, he doubted he could make the ascent half so well.

He gave it his best try. He grabbed the rope, made a run for the fence, leapt into the air, and pulled with all his might. He scrambled over, then thudded down on the other side. He was less graceful than the Old Man, but he made it.

They had violated the primary Law of the Sentinel. They had entered the forest outside the wall.

They were in the territory of the Creepers.

The Old Man retrieved his rope and quickly put it back in his pack.

He still couldn't believe it. He was outside the village walls for the first time in his life. A surge of excitement raced through his body, but it was soon replaced by another feeling altogether. "We will be dead in minutes."

The Old Man scanned the forest. "I know a few tricks." He ran a few feet, holding a finger to his lips, signaling him to be quiet.

They listened to the Black Sentry on the other side of the fence.

"Where did they go?" he heard one Sentry ask.

A few of them must have suspected where they'd gone, but no one spoke the words. Probably they feared that if they suggested their quarry had gone over the fence, they might be ordered to follow.

The Sentry moved along the fence. Their voices became more distant. He felt safe for a fleeting instant.

Then he detected the faintest rustling behind them. Within the forest.

"Creepers," he whispered, barely able to form the horrible word.

"Follow me," the Old Man said.

He turned, wondering whether the Old Man would move left or right. To his surprise, he did neither. He moved up.

The Old Man grabbed a nearby tree by its lowest branch and hoisted himself aloft. Climbing trees in the Forest of the Creepers? Was he mad?

"Come on!" the Old Man hissed, hauling himself up to the next branch.

He followed. Pressing his foot against the trunk, he managed to hoist himself to the first branch. This tree seemed different than any tree he had ever seen or touched in the village. The trees he climbed as a boy were perfectly formed, perfectly smooth. But this tree was rough and asymmetrical. Bits of bark broke off in his hands. Looking around, he saw that the trees were not perfectly spaced, but were irregular, almost haphazard. The Sentinel's need for Order apparently did not reach outside the village fence.

"This tree seems . . . strange," he commented.

"That's because it's real," the Old Man replied. "You must climb higher."

Glancing up, he saw that the Old Man was a good three branches ahead of him.

He continued his ascent until he was on the same level as the Old Man.

"We should be safe. At least for a while."

"I've heard the Creepers can climb trees," he said, barely daring to think the thought.

"You've heard correctly," the Old Man replied. "When the scent of prey is upon them, they will go almost anywhere. They can whip their tendrils around branches and pull themselves up. But it is a slow business."

"I have heard they can go anywhere and do anything. That they seek out evildoers like a hound hunts a fox."

"You've heard stories invented to frighten children. If they could go anywhere, why would they not scale the fences that surround the village?"

He did not know the answer.

"Because the fences are sheer and there is nothing for them to grab onto," the Old Man continued. "They are vile creatures, to be sure, powered by a relentless hunger for flesh. But they are not invulnerable. Or invincible."

He heard a rattling, slithering, crunching noise at the foot of the tree. And then, for the first time in his life, he saw the creature that had held him in fear his entire life.

A Creeper.

Although his first instinct was to turn away, he forced himself to watch. He felt paralyzed, transfixed by the putrid horror before him. It bore no resemblance to anything he had ever seen before. It was huge and pulsing, shifting its shape with every step. Its ghoulish exterior was covered by a glassy, revolting, gelatinous skin. It had no eyes as such, but two luminous green lights protruding from each side of what must have been the monstrosity's head. It seemed neither plant nor animal, or perhaps both. It was mostly brown and green, and its outer covering was sinuous like ivy, but almost completely covered with oozing black pustules. Worst of all was its slavering, lipless mouth—an immense wet maw.

The creature slithered forward leaving a fetid black trail of slime in its wake.

Just looking at the monster made his blood run cold. The

Creeper had two limbs, or tendrils, perhaps, that writhed above it as it slithered along the ground.

How it propelled itself was not immediately apparent. Perhaps there were short legs on the underside of the body. All he knew was that it did move, and fairly quickly at that.

He gasped as he saw the Creeper's long green tendril-tail, many times the length of its body and easily long enough to strike a full-grown man in the face.

"It's the tail that kills," the Old Man explained. "Once it has you close, there's no man fast enough to escape it."

"Is it deadly?"

The Old Man nodded. "It can be. A direct hit with its stinger will produce a painful death within an hour. Even a glancing blow can cause days or weeks of sustained agony or blindness, and can produce scars and welts that never disappear." He paused. "I've seen many a good man and woman fall to the tail of a Creeper. Many a comrade."

"There are more of you? Rebels, I mean."

"Later." The Old Man's eyes focused on the ground.

The Creeper stopped just beneath their tree. He watched as it moved its tentacles all around the tree.

The Creeper had detected them.

"What can we do?"

The Old Man did not answer. He searched the neighboring trees, but none was close enough to reach. They could jump down, but they could not jump far enough to escape the Creeper's whip-like tail. There was nothing they could do.

They were trapped.

CHAPTER

# EIGHT

Daman watched the Creeper slither around the tree, whirling its tentacles. Its tail suddenly lashed out, faster than his eye could follow. It grabbed the lowest branch of the tree, just as they had done.

He watched in terrified amazement as the quivering creature hoisted itself into the air.

There were no higher branches to which they could climb.

The Creeper waved its tendrils, targeting the next branch. If it mounted that branch, it would be close enough to strike them with its tail.

He was being punished, he thought, just as he was warned he would be. He had violated the Laws and Ways of the Sentinel by blaspheming, aiding the Old Man, and crossing the village fence. Now he would pay the penalty. He had been a fool and now he would die for it. Worse, this Old Man, who had lived so long, would come to a futile, pointless death.

He started to ask the Old Man a question, but the man silenced him with a harsh look.

He heard loud laughter from the other side of the fence.

Probably to relieve their anxiety, the Sentry were telling tales—loud, boisterous jokes.

Just as the Creeper prepared to grasp the second branch, it stopped. Its front tentacles circled around and reached out toward the fence.

The creature paused for a moment, then descended. It hit the ground in a matter of seconds and slithered toward the fence.

Had the Creeper determined that the victims over there were more attractive than the two in the tree? The insurmountable fence that stood between it and its new prey apparently did not register.

"The Creeper has no eyes, not as we do," the Old Man whispered. "It sees with its frontal antennae. And it does not have true sight. It only touches and hears and detects motion." The Creeper whirled its tail into the air, but it was not long enough to reach the top of the fence.

The Creeper hit the fence, pounding with its tentacles, making it sway. The Sentry fell silent.

He heard one of them hiss the word "Creeper."

After more than a minute of the incessant pounding, he heard the Sentry bolt down the road, away from the swaying fence and the horrible slithering and slathering sounds.

"This is our chance." As quietly as possible, the Old Man scrambled down the tree. Daman followed, quickly if clumsily. To his embarrassment, the Old Man made much better time. They both landed on the ground in a clump of something dry and crisp.

The Old Man winced. "Hurt my ankle," he whispered. But they could not discuss the matter further.

The pounding on the fence ceased. The Creeper detected their movement.

They raced back toward the fence at a point far south of the

Creeper. He knew now how quickly the hideous creature could move. They had no time to waste. The Old Man had trouble keeping up. He favored his right foot. Each step appeared to cause great pain.

He pulled the rope out of the Old Man's pack and slung the hook onto the fence. He sprang up and, balancing at the top, offered a hand to the Old Man.

"Hurry!" Out of the corner of his eye, he saw the Creeper slither closer.

After considerable effort, they landed together on the other side, barely seconds before the Creeper arrived.

They were safe, at least for the moment. The Black Sentry platoon was gone. Twilight had fallen. He knew it soon would be dark and they could travel more safely. He allowed the Old Man to place one arm around his shoulder. Together, they hobbled back toward the village.

"That dry, crackling brush we fell in on the other side of the fence," he asked. "Those were leaves?"

"They certainly were," the Old Man said, breathing heavily.

"They fall from trees?"

"Every year."

"But in the village, leaves never fall. They stay on the branches forever, in an orderly fashion."

"The Sentinel's trees are fakes, fabricated. Just like the flowers and the butterflies and . . . well, everything else in your village."

"What do you mean? A tree is a tree."

"You have a lot to learn, son."

He took the Old Man back to the village and headed for his family's home. Fortunately, the streets were mostly empty and they had ample warning before the rare traveler approached. He assumed that most people, still exhausted from the Festival the day before, had eaten their dinners and gone to bed. Still, he kept his eyes and ears alert, ready to hide at a moment's notice.

The quiet intensified his anxiety. His hands trembled with fear. He only hoped the Old Man could not detect it.

They took the road to his family's house and, as usual, began counting. As his home came into sight, a warm glow passed over him. They were actually going to make it.

Then he heard a noise almost directly behind them. Someone approached quickly.

Dragging the Old Man along, he darted into the easement beside the Moore cottage and ducked behind the trough.

Peering over the top, he tried to see who approached, hoping it was not a member of the Black Sentry. As the figure came closer, he realized it was someone smaller, younger . . .

Brita. Even in the darkness, her vibrant yellow hair seemed as radiant as the sun.

She appeared to be staring directly at them. Was it his imagination, or had she spotted them?

Barely a second later, a Black Sentry platoon marched down the lane in formation. He ducked his head and waited for them to pass. They moved slowly, obviously searching for something. Or someone.

He realized that although he might have eluded the Sentry for the moment, the search had not been abandoned.

After a few minutes, the Sentry passed out of sight.

Brita had also disappeared.

As far as he could tell, the way was clear. He helped the Old Man to his feet and quickly completed the journey to his home.

Many years before, his father had dug out a large cellar behind their house, principally for the storage of supplies and equipment and baking ingredients.

The perfect place to hide the Old Man.

They crept inside. He tried to make the Old Man comfortable. He could see the man was in pain.

"I will fetch the physic."

"No. You must tell no one I am here."

"But your ankle—"

"It's a minor injury. It will heal on its own in time."

"The physic is a good man."

The Old Man shook his head. "The Sentinel's influence is everywhere. There is no one we can trust while he holds the villages in his grasp."

"But you can't stay here forever."

"As soon as my ankle is strong again, I will be on my way. I have a quest to complete."

The Old Man spoke bravely, but as he gazed into those tired eyes, as he watched the Old Man's lungs heave, he found it difficult to believe the man could carry on much longer.

"I will return later with pillows and bedding to make you more comfortable."

The Old Man smiled. His face drew up, intensifying the crinkles around his eyes. "You are a good boy. And a brave one. Thank you."

He lit a small candle and hurried out of the cellar, careful that no one should see him.

WHEN DAMAN ENTERED the front door, he found his mother waiting for him.

"Where have you been?"

"I—I was—" What could he say? "I was . . . delivering bread for Father."

"You have been gone eight times as long as your task required."

"I'm sorry, Mother. I was—" He stopped, drew in his breath. He couldn't tell her the truth, but he didn't want to lie, either.

"Idling at the marketplace?"

"No."

"You weren't at your practice session with Mykah. He came looking for you."

"No . . ."

"Making merry at Victor's celebration?"

"No." He wanted her to know that he had not been wasting his time. But he could not explain. She was upset enough already. How could he tell her he had aided someone the Acolyte himself had named an enemy of the Sentinel?

"Yes, Mother," he said finally. "That's what I was doing." He hoped she didn't check with any of those who were at the victory celebration. "I'm sorry."

His mother's anger was palpable. Her hands tightened and her nails bit into his shoulder. "You will go straight to your room."

"Yes, Mother."

"You will have no supper tonight. Or tomorrow. You will not be permitted to see your friends for"—her voice trembled—"until I say so. Except Mykah, of course. You may work for your father and prepare for the Winnowing. And that is all! Do you understand me?"

"Yes, Mother."

———

Daman went through the usual motions of preparing for bed, even though he had no intention of sleeping. Just before he turned down his bed, he spotted his father in the doorway.

"I have just spoken with your mother," he whispered.

"I know I've made her angry. I know she does not like me very much."

"Oh, Daman." His father pulled his boy close and hugged him again. "Your mother loves you more than she loves life. She's not angry. She's frightened."

His father did not say any more, nor was there any need. He was fifteen, soon to be sixteen. The Laws and Ways of the Sentinel could not be avoided.

"I will try to do better," he whispered into his father's ear. "I promise."

His father held him at arms length and smiled. "Thank you, son. I knew you would."

His father kissed his boy on the forehead and sent him to bed.

He lay in the dark, a million conflicting thoughts running through his head. What should he do? Follow the path of the Sentinel and devote himself to preparations for Winnowing? If he turned in the Old Man now, there was a chance he might escape punishment. But the Old Man would not. And some of the things the Old Man said, some of the things he only hinted at . . .

They both intrigued—and troubled him.

What should he do?

———

DAMAN LAY in his darkened room, not letting his eyes close, until he was certain everyone else in the house was asleep. He crawled out of bed, collected a few items, and crept down into the cellar, using a candle for illumination. He thought he might find the Old Man asleep, but he was just as alert as when he left.

He gave his guest a pillow and some blankets. The Old Man

wrapped himself in them and seemed pleased, although he noted that the trembling did not subside.

"Do you not need sleep?"

The Old Man shook his head. "When you get to be my age, my young friend, you sleep very little. And I confess my foot still causes me some pain."

"Are you sure—"

"I'll be fine."

He reached into the pockets of his coat. "I brought you some food from the larder." He looked up suddenly. "You do still eat, don't you?"

Again he witnessed the man's warm smile. "Yes, my friend. I still eat."

He noticed that, despite all the exercise they'd had earlier, and the fact that the Old Man must not have eaten for some time, he took small bites and ultimately ate very little. He did not seem to have much appetite.

A moment later, the Old Man stopped eating abruptly. "What was that?"

He froze. Behind them, he heard a creaking sound. It was the outer door to the cellar . . . opening.

Someone was coming.

CHAPTER

# NINE

Daman blew out the candle and dove behind a shelf filled with jars. He froze, barely breathing, watching the cellar door. The Old Man crawled out of sight.

The door opened, then quietly closed. After a moment's hesitation, a slender figure stepped through the opening carrying a small candle of her own.

Brita wore a dark hooded cloak that covered her clothes and her hair, but hers was a face he would recognize anywhere.

"Daman?" she said, barely above a whisper. "Where are you?"

He didn't answer. He didn't know what to do.

"Daman?" she repeated, stepping into the cellar. "I saw you come in."

He knew she would not leave until she had searched the room and discovered the Old Man. "I'm here." He stepped out from behind the cluttered shelf. "What are you doing?"

"I'm looking for your companion."

"I don't know what you're talking about."

"Don't play the fool with me, Daman. I'm much smarter than you. I saw you with him in the street. I tried to warn you that the Black Sentry was coming."

He thought back to when they hid behind the trough. He realized that if it had not been for her arrival, they probably would have been discovered.

"Where is he?" she said, stepping down off the steps.

"He's gone," he said hastily. "I don't know where he is now."

"Daman," she said firmly, "please stop these pathetic attempts to mislead me. You're a horrible liar."

"I . . . can't take the risk."

"Daman, think. I know it's difficult for you, but try. If I'd wanted to inform the Black Sentry, I would've done so already. They'd be with me now. And I wouldn't have tried to help you outside."

"I meant, I can't risk . . . involving you."

"Too late. I'm already involved, and I want to help."

"Why?"

"Because I know you're not smart enough to do it alone. Now where is he?"

"I'm here." Before he could prevent it, the Old Man revealed himself. "May I ask why you seek to help me?"

"You're the one the Acolyte spoke of, aren't you? The Rebel."

The Old Man's eyes appraised her carefully before he answered. "I suppose I must be."

"You're a member of the Resistance."

"You know of the Resistance?"

"Obviously."

A tiny smile played on the Old Man's lips. "What would you know about it?"

"Are you still fighting? Recruiting new members?"

He had no idea what they were talking about, but he remained silent and tried to learn.

"We must fight for the greater good," the Old Man said. "We must never stop fighting."

Brita came very close to him. "I want to join you."

"What?"

"I want to join the Resistance. I want to help you."

He stepped between them. "Brita, think what you're saying. The Laws and Ways of the Sentinel do not—"

"Be quiet, Daman." She turned back to the Old Man. "I want to go with you. And I want to go now."

The thought of her leaving the village left him strangely unsettled. "You have obligations here, Brita. You will soon be assigned a mate. Perhaps even . . . Mykah . . ."

"That's the point. Part of it, anyhow."

The Old Man raised a shaggy eyebrow. "You do not want to marry this . . . Mykah?"

"No, I don't."

"Is there something wrong with Mykah?"

"No. He's adequate, in his way. Everyone says he'll be Magistrate one day."

"Then what is your objection?"

"I'm barely sixteen. There's so much I want to do, so much I want to see."

"But surely—"

"If I wed Mykah, my life will be over. I'll be his wife, and the bearer of his children, and nothing more. I'll have no rights under the Sentinel's Laws. No ability to make my own decisions. No power to control my own destiny."

"But that is the Sentinel's Way," Daman said, even though her objections to Mykah did not altogether displease him. "It's how life is. It's how it has always been."

"It may be how it is," the Old Man said firmly, "but it is definitely not how it has always been." He took Brita's hand and drew her beside him. "I appreciate your courage, young woman, but you have no idea the dangers that would confront you if you joined me."

"Nonetheless, it's what I want."

"Plus," he continued, "as much as I would like a companion, I fear you would only slow me down—without providing any assistance."

"I could help you," she insisted.

"Have you some special skills? Do you know how to pick locks?"

"No."

"Do you know the secret trails that can take you from one village to the next without encountering the Black Sentry?"

"No."

"Do you have weapons? Money?"

"No, no."

He patted her on the shoulder. "I admire your courage, but—"

"I can read."

Her words flew out and hovered, suspended in the silence.

Daman gaped. Surely she had not said what he thought she said.

The Old Man gazed at Brita. "What did you say?"

"I said I can read."

"But that's impossible."

"It's true."

Daman barely knew what the word meant. *Read?* What was this *read?* All he knew for certain was that it was forbidden by the Sentinel.

"But how did you learn?"

Brita raised her chin. "My mother has books."

"Books are forbidden." He knew that, although he didn't truly understand what books were.

"Nonetheless, she has them, and she brings them out, late

at night, and she taught me to read them. I have read many books. That's why I'm so much smarter than the other young people in the village."

"Books . . . make people smart?"

"Indeed they do," the Old Man said. "Which is why the Sentinel has forbidden them. Where did your mother get these books, Brita?"

"From her grandmother. Who got them from her aunt. Who got them from her mother."

It seemed his father's Watch was not the only relic being handed down through the generations.

"They all defied the Sentinel?"

"In secret, yes. Not everyone in the villages loves and obeys the Sentinel. Not everyone believes."

"I am glad to hear it," the Old Man said. "I had all but given up hope. What about you, son? Are you also interested in joining the Resistance?"

"I have never before heard of this Resistance," he answered. And yet, even though he couldn't explain why, he knew the Resistance was a force for good. And he wanted to be a part of it. "But yes. I wish to join."

"But why?"

"I—I can't explain." He knew it sounded feeble, but it was the best he could manage. "I just know it's the right thing to do."

The Old Man's white eyebrows drew closer together. "Is it possible . . ." he said, more to himself than to the others. He shook his head. "Let me tell you about the Resistance. It explains my current, simple quest. To deliver this."

He reached inside his tunic, and a moment later, withdrew a glittering red stone tied to a leather strap that hung around his neck.

The stone was smooth and irregularly shaped, like a glittering gemstone. It shone in the candlelight.

"Is it . . . some kind of jewel?"

"No, son," the Old Man replied. "Although it is beautiful, it's not a thing of nature. It's a thing of man."

"But what is it?" Brita seemed entranced by the glittering object.

"It's a key. A unique key. Not a jewel, and yet more valuable than any jewel—at least to us. This stone, and the others like it, are the only powers in the world that can defeat the Sentinel. That's why he had them hidden. It has taken the Resistance more than a hundred years to find this one. And now that we have it, we believe that, for the first time since the Sentinel clutched the world in his steely grip—he is worried."

"How does the key work?"

"That I do not know." He tucked it back inside his tunic. "My friend Matthew knew more, but he was captured by the Black Sentry. I must return this to the other Rebels. They will know what to do with it."

"And where are these rebels?" Brita asked. "Are they in Merrindale?"

"Of course not. I must take the key on a journey. But the Sentry spotted me outside this village and now I don't know how to get it out safely." He smiled faintly. "And as kind and courageous as you two are, I do not think you can solve my problem."

The cellar fell silent. He was not sure what to do or say.

Brita broke the silence. "You said that things have not always been as they are now. That there was a time when girls had other choices."

"Everyone did," the Old Man replied.

"You speak of the time of the Ancients," Daman said. "But

we've been taught that before the Sentinel ruled, the world was evil and chaotic. The Constructs ruled."

"That is not so," the Old Man answered. "True, at times, there was chaos. Humans are by nature imperfect, disorderly. Competitive. But even so, the old days were better times. Freer times."

"You lived then? Before the Sentinel?"

"Oh no. This was long before I was born. But I have heard tales about those times."

"And I have read about them," Brita added.

"How do we know that you're telling the truth?" Daman asked. "How do we know that these are not just . . . stories?"

"In a sense, we cannot *know*," the Old Man admitted. "I cannot prove it to you. You must have faith. You must believe."

There was a pause. "I do believe," he whispered.

The Old Man gazed at him once again with intense interest.

"Tell us more," Brita urged.

The Old Man nodded. "There are others who could tell you more. I know the general course of events, though not many of the details. But there was a time when all people were free, when freedom was so common that people rarely thought of it and often took it for granted. It was a time of wonders. A time when men and women could pursue their highest and best destiny."

"Everyone was free to choose—for themselves?" he said. "To make their own decisions?"

"Do you find that incredible, Daman?"

"I should," he said softly. "But no, I don't. I've had . . . dreams."

"What kind of dreams?"

"I can't explain it." He shook his head rapidly. "Tell us more about the world of the past."

"It was a world of many great achievements. But there were

some who disliked this world. Freedom led to disorder, inefficiency. Chaos. And at times, madness. These people wanted to reshape the world in a more orderly, predictable, controlled image. And the greatest of these was the Sentinel."

"Where did the Sentinel come from?"

"I do not know. Some say he is the physical manifestation of our worst fears. Some say he is pure intellect, fulfilling a single-minded purpose. Some say the Sentinel descended from the skies. I do not know the answer. All I know is that the Sentinel acquired great power, and by using it, he was able to make all the Constructs, all over the land, stop working."

This puzzled him. "But that was a blessing, wasn't it? The Constructs were our enemies."

"The Constructs were neither friends nor enemies. They were tools. Oh, they could be used for evil purposes, as any tool can. But it was the person operating the machine that was evil, not the machine."

"I have seen the machines!" he said, struggling to make sense of this. "The Acolyte showed us one in the Arena, and it was a hideous, evil thing."

The Old Man shrugged. "It was a thresher."

"A—what?"

"A thresher. A device that helped farmers reap their crops," Brita replied. "I've read about them."

"Very good," the Old Man said. "Very good indeed."

He was confused. "But—we need no machines to help us farm."

"So you say," the Old Man replied. "But isn't food scarce every year, particularly during the winter? Aren't there people with too little, especially in the Nether End? Aren't there children who go to bed hungry? In the time of the Constructs, men were able to produce a thousand times as much food. There was no need for anyone to go without. Indeed, some had far too much."

That silenced him. He had seen the hungry—slaves, usually, though sometimes others. Sometimes even children.

"The Resistance wants to restore the dreams of the past, or better yet to build new ones, and to end the tyranny of the Sentinel. So far, it has been just that—a dream. But now, for the first time . . ." The Old Man gazed at the red stone dangling around his neck, then fell silent.

Daman could see that the Old Man tired and, despite earlier protestations, needed sleep.

"May I ask one more question?" Brita asked.

The Old Man's eyelids rose. "How can I deny anything to she who reads?"

"I want to know about—this." She pointed to the top of his tunic, where the white backward collar showed through. "Why do you dress in this peculiar way? I've never seen anything like it."

"I'm glad you asked," he said, "but there is more to it than I can possibly explain tonight."

"Just tell me a little, then," she urged. "Does it relate to the world before the Sentinel?"

"This is a very old costume, and a time-honored one. I wear it as a symbol, a reminder, of a time when people worshiped out of love, not fear. When people had faith that freed them, rather than enslaved them." He laid his hand gently against Brita's radiant hair. "I wear it because it gives me something to believe in. Perhaps in time it will give you something to believe in as well."

Brita pressed her hand against his.

He laid the pillow and blanket in a flat place in the back of the cellar so the Old Man would be comfortable and protected from casual view. He and Brita started up the stairs.

All at once, they heard a sudden thunderous noise outside.

Brita jumped, grabbing his shoulder. He didn't mind, but at the moment he was more concerned with determining the source of the sound.

Someone pounded on the cellar door.

"We know you're in there," they heard a voice call. "Open this door. By the order of the Black Sentry!"

Daman knew he needed to do something, but he could not think what. His brain felt as frozen as his body.

Without warning, Brita pushed him to the ground. She pulled the hood of her cloak over her head, leaned across Daman, and planted her lips directly on his.

His eyes widened with amazement.

The cellar door burst open. The blaze of torchlight illuminated the stairs.

"Who's in there?" the voice shouted. "Daman, is that you? Didn't you hear me?"

It was Mykah, in uniform, with a small platoon of Black Sentry behind him.

As soon as Mykah entered, Brita broke off the kiss, as if suddenly startled, and buried her face in the crook of his neck.

Mykah appeared puzzled. Then his eyes adjusted and he understood. What Brita wanted him to understand. The hood covered Brita's distinctive hair, but it was still obvious that Daman held a girl in his arms.

A slow smile crept across Mykah's face. "Daman, you old dog."

Awkwardly, he tried to return the smile.

"Sorry to interrupt," Mykah said, clearing his throat. "We're all searching for this Rebel the Acolyte warned us about. He was spotted in the forest today. We believe he has a local accomplice and may be hiding somewhere inside the village." He grinned. "But I can see you have concerns of your own." He laughed heartily, then moved his torch toward Brita's head. A strand of her hair tumbled out from her hood.

The expression on Mykah's face was unmistakable. But he said nothing.

He turned abruptly without a word. "Come on, men."

They left, closing the cellar door behind them.

When they were sure they were alone, Brita extracted her face from his neck. "Sorry," she said abruptly. "It was all I could think of. Hope I didn't embarrass you."

"N—no," he said clumsily. "I wasn't—I mean, I didn't—"

She pulled away before he could complete his sentence. "How are you?" she asked the Old Man.

"Even more impressed than I was before. By both of you."

He promised to check on the Old Man again in the morning and to bring food. Then they both left him to rest.

He stopped Brita before she left for home. "I will come and see you tomorrow. There are . . . matters we must discuss."

She nodded, then he quietly returned to his house and crawled beneath the warm covers of his bed. He slept heavily but not well, and once again his sleep was filled with dreams—dreams of watches and threshers and books and different times, when Constructs roamed the land and people lived without the Laws and Ways of the Sentinel.

A time of freedom.

———

Daman awoke full of energy. After dressing, he went to the kitchen to see his parents before they left for their daily business.

Xander had already set out the meal. Lieutenant Coffin's report apparently had not yet reached the Magistrate.

His parents were both at the breakfast table waiting for him. Apparently they'd been awake for some time.

He hoped his mother had softened, or forgotten about his punishment, but he soon saw that was not the case. One stony look from her was sufficient to tell him his sins had not been forgiven.

"I said last night you were to have no supper," she said, through stiff, tense lips.

"Yes, Mother."

"Yet when I went to the larder this morning, I found a loaf and a rind of cheese missing. Can you explain this?"

In fact, he had eaten nothing. The missing food was what he had taken to the Old Man.

His father studiously watched them both.

"You took that food," his mother pronounced. "Didn't you, Daman?"

He nodded.

With unexpected ferocity, she grabbed him by both arms and shook him violently. "When will you grow up, Daman? When will you learn to follow instructions? *Why can't you do as you are told?*"

And then, as quickly as the rage had begun, it ended. She pushed away from him and pressed one hand to her forehead. A moment later, he was shocked to see his own mother crying.

She tried to regain control but couldn't. Finally she fled the room, tears streaming from her face.

As if he didn't feel badly enough already, he felt his father's eyes boring down on him.

His father placed a roll on a plate with a small piece of cured meat. "Eat your breakfast."

He did. They sat in silence, and it was perhaps because of the silence that he became immediately aware of the tumult outside.

Even with the door closed he could tell that something was happening. He heard confusion, running, arguing.

"The Black Sentry is everywhere today," his father explained. "The Acolyte's private platoon has remained with him here and taken control of our local Sentry. They've blanketed the village. They're determined to find this Rebel."

He tried not to react. "Really?"

"Apparently they came close to catching him last night, but someone helped him escape."

He tried not to seem overly interested. "I'm surprised that anyone in the village would help a Rebel escape."

"No doubt the Sentry were surprised as well." His father paused a moment. "Some reports I've heard claim a young boy helped the Rebel escape."

"Surely not."

His father paused. "I can't help but remember that you were out late last night, Daman."

"I was at a party. Victor's celebration."

"So I heard." He looked at his son with a strong and unbroken gaze. "I don't suppose you heard anything about this Rebel?"

"No one said a word to me about him."

"I see." There was a long silence before his father spoke again. "Daman, you must be careful. If you do . . . hear anything about this Rebel, stay away from him. He will be dangerous. He is probably a member of the Resistance."

He could barely conceal his amazement. "You know of the Resistance?"

"Of course," his father replied. "And it seems—so do you."

He averted his eyes. "I've heard rumors. Stories, that's all. I suppose you've heard the stories, too."

His father kept his eyes locked on his son's face. "I was a member of the Resistance."

His knife clattered to the table. "But—you—" He paused. "You're my father!"

"It was a long time ago." His father's eyes seemed distant and unfocused. "I was young. Younger than you, even. Before my Winnowing. And I was in love with a beautiful girl."

"Mother."

"No. This was well before your mother was assigned to me. This girl's name was Abigail. And she was wonderful. Smart, quick, fearless. Full of ideas. She didn't believe people should be forced to do things they hated, or that their most important decisions should be made for them. She wanted us to join the Resistance, so we did. She wanted us to defy the Sentinel, to escape from our village. We thought about it and talked about it constantly. But in the end . . ." He sighed. "It was just too difficult. I couldn't muster the . . . the strength, I suppose. The courage to turn my back on everything I had ever known, ever been taught." He fell silent.

"So what happened?"

His father shrugged. "Eventually Abigail was assigned to someone else. I lost my Winnowing, and was transported to Merrindale. Eventually I earned enough Merit to be assigned your mother, and later still, to be allowed a son."

"Father . . . do you regret your decision?"

"Of course not. We have a good life now—better than many. If I had defied the Sentinel, I would never have had this cottage, and I would never have had you—the greatest pride of my life.

And make no mistake, Daman—even if the Sentinel disapproves of displays of strong emotion—I care deeply for your mother. But," he added, after a long pause, "I've never forgotten that beautiful girl of my youth."

"Father?" Daman said at last.

"Yes?"

"Do you . . . believe in the Sentinel?"

A deep furrow crossed his forehead. "What do you mean? Do I believe he exists? Yes, of course he does."

"But the other night when you showed me your . . . treasure and we talked and—I just wondered. Do you believe?" He struggled to find the right words. "Do you believe in the Laws and Ways? Do you believe that the life the Sentinel demands is the best?"

"Suggesting otherwise is heresy. The Black Sentry could take you away, could take all of us away, and our belongings, just for asking the question."

"Yes, Father. I know that. Will you answer my question?"

His father's lips pursed. "There's nothing wrong with being a baker, you know. It's an honorable trade. But it's not what I wanted to do. I wanted to be an inventor."

"An inventor?" He wasn't sure what the word meant.

"I wanted to make things—wonderful things. Like the Watch I showed you."

"Constructs?"

"If you insist on calling them that. I wanted to make people's lives better, to ease their labor, with my creations."

He nodded. "You would've been a good inventor, Father."

"There is much about the Sentinel's world that is good. Order eases many burdens. Eliminates complications. Strife. Inequity. Uncertainty. And yet . . . sometimes at night, I long for the freedom to explore my own path, to make my own way. To fulfill my own dreams." He looked up abruptly. "I hate the way we live, Daman. I hate the Sentinel and his world. I hate everything about it."

"Then why—"

"The Sentinel is all-powerful. We do not have the strength to resist him. None of us do."

"But if the Res—"

His father rose suddenly. "It's foolish to speak of such things. Resistance is impossible. Look what's happened to this poor Rebel and all those like him, running from village to village, never safe, always a short step from execution. No. The Sentinel's Way is the only Way."

His father left for the bakery. He knew his mother expected him to follow, to spend the day helping, until it was time to practice again for the Winnowing. But he did not.

———

CAREFUL THAT NO one was watching, Daman made his way to the cellar and crept through the doors. The Old Man was wide-awake. He held a piece of parchment before him, studying it intently.

Was this a book? he wondered. Was the man reading? But as he stepped quietly forward, he saw that the parchment bore pictures—irregular shapes in various colors and sizes.

"Is that a book?" he asked.

"Oh no—it's a map."

Once again, he had to struggle with an unfamiliar concept. "I've never heard of them."

"Forbidden by the Sentinel," the Old Man said. "Who needs them? No one's allowed to go anywhere. At least not on their own initiative."

The fact that it was forbidden by the Sentinel only made it more interesting. "Is that something you . . . read?"

"In a way. But it isn't made up of words, not primarily. It's a picture. It helps you find your way. It's how I found your village. And how I hope to get out."

"But—how?"

"The pictures represent the surrounding countryside. By looking at the map, you can locate your destination and determine how to get there. See?" He pointed at a small blue dot toward the bottom of the map. "That represents your village, Merrindale." He moved his finger upward. "This orange dot represents the nearest neighboring village, Clovis. This brown line shows the road that connects the two."

He nodded as if he understood everything, though in truth he understood almost nothing. "I suppose it must take years of practice to learn how to understand that."

The Old Man laughed. "Not at all. A bright boy like you—I bet you could learn it in ten minutes. Would you like that?"

He scooted forward. "Very much."

The Old Man explained the mysterious workings of the map, teaching him about north, south, east, and west, about relative scale, about orientation. Before long, he understood the basic principles.

"That's wonderful. Almost . . . magical. Where did you get this map?"

"It was given to me by another member of the Resistance. Where he got it, I don't know. We've made an ongoing effort to reclaim the relics of the past. Sometimes they help us in our work. And sometimes we keep them because . . . well, just because. Because someone should."

He gazed at some of the other locations on the Map. There were so many places—some he knew by reputation, some he'd never heard of before. The Forest of Savages. Ingrid Pass. Elliott's Creek. And he was particularly mesmerized by dark markings surrounding Merrindale. The Old Man explained that they were words, and that the words read: HERE THERE BE CREEPERS.

He couldn't believe there were so many places in the world —so many places he'd never seen. He wanted to visit them all —now more than ever.

He pointed to the orange circle representing Clovis. "It must be much bigger than Merrindale."

"Yes," the Old Man agreed. "The largest in this region. The Sentinel does not allow his villages to become any larger. Not in any of the regions."

"Why not?"

The Old Man shrugged. "I could only speculate. The larger a town grows, the more people are packed together in one space, the more difficult they become to control." The Old Man rolled up the map. "Can you think of a good hiding place? For the map and the key? Just in case."

He scanned the cellar. Under the supplies? On the top shelf? He shook his head. If the Sentry searched, they would find them in minutes.

He thought harder. The Sentry might look under and over things—but they probably would not look inside them. Say, inside a burlap bag filled with flour. Who would?

Daman took the two treasures and buried them deep within the largest bag, then retied the top.

"They should be safe now. As safe as they'll be anywhere." He shifted awkwardly. "I should probably go. My father expects me at the bakery."

"Of course. You must do everything you would normally do. Don't create suspicion. My ankle feels better. Tonight, under the cover of darkness, I'll try to escape."

He knew that was best. The Old Man needed to proceed with his work, to get that Key back to the people who could use it. But at the same time, the thought of the Old Man departing saddened him.

"I have one favor to ask you, Daman. There is a man I know who, last I heard, had been transported to Merrindale. Do you know a man called Martin Adkins?"

"My father?"

The Old Man grinned. "Indeed. I'm not surprised. He also had . . . a Gift." He paused. "You favor your father, Daman. Perhaps in more ways than you realize."

The Old Man squeezed his shoulder. "Run along now. I'll see you tonight."

———

As Daman made his way through the village, he found the tumult had intensified. The Black Sentry were everywhere. They were harsh and insolent, bowling people over in their desperation to find the Old Man. They broke into homes and shops, stopping passersby and searching them. He felt sorry for these innocents—and guilty, too. He knew that if the Sentry did not find their quarry soon, it would be even worse for the people of Merrindale.

At the same time, he worried about the Old Man's safety. He had deflected the Black Sentry from the cellar for now, but as the search intensified, they would surely return.

He knew he should report to his father's shop, but instead, he headed toward Brita's house. If the Old Man was going to escape, he knew she would want to help. He wondered if she would still be determined to join the Resistance after seeing the frenzy the Black Sentry were creating.

He found Mykah standing just outside Brita's cottage.

Mykah stiffened. He didn't have to guess why. "Daman,

have you seen Brita? She was supposed to meet me this morning. We've been summoned by the Magistrate."

He knew what that meant. He assumed Brita would be assigned to be his wife. But didn't he recognize her in the cellar last night? If so, he chose not to mention it. "I was told there was a chance we would be counseled by the Acolyte himself. And now I can't find her."

He wasn't surprised. He remembered what Brita said the night before about the prospect of marriage. "Did you check her home?"

"Of course I did. There was no answer. She must've gone somewhere. How could she forget?"

"The village is chaotic today. Perhaps she's somewhere safe with her parents."

"You may be right. I'll check her father's mill." Mykah started to go, then stopped. "Daman," he said slowly, "you've known Brita almost as long as I have."

"That's true."

"Has she seemed . . . odd to you of late?"

He felt himself coloring. Was this a veiled reference to what Mykah witnessed in the cellar? "Odd in what way?"

"I don't know. I can't explain it. When I talk to her . . . it's as if she's somewhere else altogether."

He had no response for him. None that he dared utter, anyway.

"Well, I must go," Mykah said. "I have to finish this appointment, so I can rejoin the search. Every member of the Sentry has been called, no matter how young or inexperienced. This Rebel is a great enemy of the Sentinel, you know. It is said that the man who finds him will be elevated to the highest ranks." He leaned in conspiratorially and whispered. "We think someone in the village is hiding him."

He tried to appear astonished. "Surely not."

"Don't worry. Regardless of who finds him, this heretic will be punished. And," Mykah added, "anyone hiding him will die."

# ELEVEN

As Daman considered what to do next—he heard a faint tapping from inside the cottage.

He turned slowly, trying not to attract attention. The tapping came from the window.

Brita was at home, after all. Trying to get his attention.

He approached the front door as if doing nothing out of the ordinary. An instant before his hand touched the knocker, the door swung open before him.

No one was visible in the entryway.

He stepped inside.

The door closed behind him. Brita huddled behind the door.

"Mykah is looking for you," he said.

"Do you think I don't know that? Don't be such an imbecile." She stepped away from the door, motioning for him to follow her. They sat on the floor in the rearmost room of the house where they could not be seen from the street. "That's why I don't want anyone to know I'm here."

Her parents were not at home. The two of them were alone together. Another violation of the Laws and Ways of the

Sentinel. Just the thought of it made his heart beat faster. "But —why miss your appointment? Why avoid Mykah?"

"I avoided Mykah because I have no intention of marrying him, as I believe I've already told you. And I missed my appointment because we have far more urgent tasks today."

He could not help but notice her use of the word "we." "Such as?"

"We must get the Old Man out of the village."

"To where?"

"How would I know? Neither of us has ever been beyond the village fence."

Not entirely true after yesterday's adventure, but he did not correct her. "I know what lies outside the village. I've seen a map." He told her of his experience that morning with the Old Man. He also told her where he had hidden the map and the red key. "The Old Man said he intends to slip out tonight."

She nodded. "Anywhere would be safer than here."

"Is it still your intention to go with the Old Man? To join his Resistance?"

"Yes. If he'll have me."

"But think of the dangers. The Black Sentry. The Creepers. The Savages."

"I would rather die aiding the Resistance than die trapped in this village, living an empty life married to Mykah."

"You should think carefully before you do anything that dangerous."

"These are odd words coming from the boy who rescued the Old Man."

"I . . . would not want you to come to any harm."

"I do not intend to come to any harm."

They sat quietly for an awkward moment. "Brita . . . is what you said true?"

"About what?"

"About books."

The corners of her lips turned up. "Would you like to see one?"

"Very much."

She glanced at the door again, making sure they were out of sight. Then she tossed aside the area rug in the center of the room. She inserted three fingers into what appeared to be a knothole in a plank of the wooden floor. To his astonishment, the plank rose out of its groove.

"We keep them in this hideaway, where even the Black Sentry won't look. I only wish it were large enough to hide the Old Man."

She reached into the opening, stretching her arm almost to its fullest extent. A moment later, she withdrew what he could only assume was a book. It was about the size of a loaf of bread, but black and thick. The outer covering was heavy, while inside, many thin sheets—what Brita called "pages"—were packed together.

He crouched beside her. These pages were covered, in part with pictures, but mostly with tiny scratchings similar to those he saw on the map. He could make no sense of them. "What do you do with it?"

"You read it," she replied.

"I don't understand."

She pointed at the page. "These are letters. They form words. The words form sentences, just as we do when we talk."

"And you can read these scratches?"

"Of course I can."

"What do they tell you?"

"Stories, sometimes."

"About events that happened before the time of the Sentinel?"

"Sometimes."

"What else do the books say?"

"Some recount the lives of great men and women. Or explain how things worked. How people lived. This book is"—she turned its spine so he could see the word—"an ency-clo-pe-dia. Sailing dash Tunis."

"What does that mean?"

She frowned. "I'm not sure. But the book tells of many wondrous things." Her eyes lit. "Of termites and threshers and a man called Shakespeare who wrote poems."

"Poems?"

"Poems are words arranged so that— Oh, it's too difficult to explain. But they're beautiful! And so are the stories."

"Are there many of these . . . poems? Or stories?"

"There were. Before the Sentinel forbid them."

"If they were beautiful, why would the Sentinel forbid them?"

"My mother says it's because they put ideas into people's minds. New and different ideas. The Sentinel wants everyone to have the same ideas. The ones he gave them." She clutched the book close to her. "There's so much out there, Daman. So much we know nothing about."

He saw the happiness these books brought her. He was glad —but also sorry he could not share this delight. "How many books do you have?"

"Seven. We used to have eight, but the pages in one became brittle and crumbled into dust. Mother says we must be careful with those that remain. We take the books out less and less now."

She showed him the other books hidden under the floor. All had scratchings he did not understand. One said "ALMANAC," one was the story of a man named "LINCOLN," with pictures, one was a storybook about "JUSTICE," one was a very thick book about "SCIENCE," and another was the book Brita said she understood least of all, something called "THE HOLY BIBLE" written by a man named Gideon.

"This book is a wonderful account of the Ancients' government," she said. "From the time when people controlled their own destinies and animals could talk."

He blinked. "Animals could talk?"

"Of course," she said scornfully. "Didn't you know?"

His forehead creased. He knew she was more knowledgeable than he, but . . . "It's hard to imagine a time when animals could speak."

"Only for you," she scoffed. "Because you are so unlearned. The proof is right here. This book tells all about it." She showed him the thin volume, which she explained was called *Animal Farm*. "The Time of the Ancients was a time of wonders."

Finally, she showed him a book called a "dictionary," which she explained was the key to understanding the words in the other books.

"If you see a word and you don't know what it means, you can look it up in the dictionary."

"But if you don't know the word, how can you look it up?"

"By how it's spelled."

"What?" He didn't begin to understand. He was so lost he couldn't even ask intelligent questions. "Brita," he whispered, "do you think perhaps . . . I could learn to read these scratches?"

"Of course you could. You don't have to be smart. You just have to know how it works."

"What is . . . SCIENCE?"

She scooped up the thick book. "Oh, that's my favorite. It has so many great ideas. Things you would never imagine." She paused a moment, scrutinizing his face, as if determining whether she could trust him. "Would you like to see my experiment?"

"What is that?"

"That's when you try to discover or prove something with a test."

"Like what?"

"Anything. Why the world works the way it does."

"We were taught that the world works the way it does because the Sentinel wishes it so."

She apparently didn't deem that remark even worthy of reply. "This isn't my first experiment. I made a compass, once, with a needle and a small pan of water. And I've watched mold grow on old bread. Did you know that hot air rises?"

"I'm . . . not sure what you mean."

"Then just stay silent and watch. Maybe you'll learn something." She removed some materials from the back corner of a cabinet. She took a length of fabric, maybe twice the size of the book, then started a small fire in the open hearth. Once the kindling caught on, she held the fabric over the flames, then rounded the cloth like a ball. To Daman's surprise, the cloth held the round shape, even after she removed it from the hearth.

"It looks as if it were solid," he remarked.

"Well, in a way, it is. It's filled with the hot air rising from the fire. Now watch this." She sealed the fabric, tying it with a string, then brought it into the front room and released it.

It rose toward the ceiling.

His lips parted. "It's amazing."

"It's a balloon," she said, laughing. "And it isn't amazing— it's science. I love balloons. I've read all about them."

"Did the Ancients have balloons?"

"Of course. They were so common they became toys for children. The Ancients had even more amazing machines that flew through the air. Machines so strong people could take long rides covering enormous distances in a short time. They could travel all over the world."

"But—why?"

"To see what there was to see," she said softly. "To see the world outside their own village."

"Brita, do you believe everything the Old Man told us? About the world of the past?"

"I do. Do you?"

He paused. "Sometimes at night I have strange . . . well, I call them dreams, but they aren't really dreams. Because I'm not asleep. I guess I don't really see them—they just sort of appear in my mind. Things I've never seen with my eyes. I don't know where they come from, or why, but I do know—"

He heard a terrific commotion in the street outside the house. Hurriedly, she hid the books and all traces of her experiment in the hiding place under the floor. After she finished, he stepped outside to see what was happening.

Dozens of villagers scrambled to get out of the way. A Black Sentry platoon rushed past in formation.

He felt a cold clutching at his heart. What could be happening?

Xander rushed toward him, calling his name. His instinctive reaction was outrage. A slave should only speak when spoken to. He admired what Xander had done the day before, but surely insolence such as this—

"Daman," Xander said, "come quick!" He breathed so heavily he could barely speak.

"Xander, please conduct yourself in—"

"It's the Black Sentry."

"What about them?"

"They've found the Rebel. The one the Acolyte spoke of!.

He tried not to react. "What has this to do with me?"

"Don't you understand? They found him at your house. While your father was at home."

"My father would never help an enemy of the Sentinel."

"The Black Sentry think he did. They have your house surrounded. And your father is trapped inside."

Daman didn't wait to hear any more. He raced past Xander, tearing down the street toward home.

His home was surrounded by the Black Sentry, perhaps forty or more of them, more than he had ever seen in one place at any time.

"Mister Adkins," the Captain of the Guard shouted through the open window. "You are commanded to come out of your house. By order of the Black Sentry!"

A hush fell over the street as everyone listened for his reply.

Nothing came.

What was his father doing? He must've been as astonished as anyone when the Sentry pulled the Old Man out of the cellar. Was he afraid to come out? Or was there something more going on?

"If you do not come forth immediately," the Captain bellowed, "we will be forced to come in after you."

Still no reply.

Grimacing, the Captain of the Guard hit the door shoulder first, then bounced back into the street. The door barely moved.

The door must've been barricaded on the other side. Rubbing his sore shoulder, the Captain motioned for several of his Sentry to join him.

Together, they exerted their combined strength on the door. Slowly but surely, it gave way. When the opening was sufficiently wide, they poured into the front room of his house.

The spectators surged forward, craning for a better view. He wormed his way through the pack and pushed his way to the open window. Most of the people in the crowd recognized him and let him pass.

Inside, his father had turned the kitchen table on its side and crouched behind it. He threw everything in sight at the intruding Sentry—firewood, fruit, even coals from the stove.

And in this manner, his father—the quiet, unassuming, mild-mannered baker—held off two platoons of the Black Sentry.

But he knew his father could not hold them back forever. Ducking and shouting, the Sentry continued to pour into the room.

From his window vantage point, he saw that his father was poised at the far end of the table, crouched down, as if preparing to spring at any moment. He could not imagine why—at first. Then he noticed the open kitchen door just beyond. The door faced an alleyway behind their house. With the Sentry drawn to the front by his father's attack, escape through the rear was a possibility.

More than twenty of the Black Sentry were in the entry of his home. If his father planned to make a run, it had to be now.

His father sprang out from behind the table, diving headlong toward the rear window.

He was fast, but the Black Sentry were faster. One had a rope with a loop at the end. It caught one of his father's legs as he made the leap, then jerked him hard back into the room. At least ten of the Sentry were on him in an instant, tying his hands and legs, beating him with their fists.

"Father!" he cried out through the window.

But there was nothing he could do. The Black Sentry had him.

# THIRTEEN

Daman broke away from the window, burrowed through the crowd, and pushed his way past the front door. Two of the Sentry grabbed him, holding him back.

"He's my father!" he shouted, but it made no difference.

Once his father was completely immobilized, the beating ceased.

"Let me go to him!" he begged, but they did not. Several others dragged his father out of the house.

Mykah was one of those dragging him away.

"Mykah," he said, "my father has treated you like his own son your entire life."

Mykah's eyes did not meet his. "I'm sorry," he said, in an odd, hollow voice. "But the Sentinel's will must be done. He's our Master."

"A Master who would do this is no Master of mine!"

A sudden, deathly quiet fell over the room. Wide eyes flitted from side to side.

Xander appeared behind him, seemingly out of nowhere. "Master, why are you out and on your feet? You know the physic said you should remain in bed. After that severe blow to your head, you are not yourself."

It took him a moment to realize what Xander was babbling about. "Oh . . . yes . . ."

Xander put his arm around his shoulder and led him out of the crowd.

Mykah and the others hauled his father away. They would take him to the Keep, where he would be held until his fate was determined at trial. But that was just a formality. He already knew what the result would be. In the entire history of the village, the Black Sentry had never once brought charges without receiving a verdict of guilty from the Magistrate. To be charged, as his father surely would be, was to be sentenced to death.

"And it was all for nothing," he heard one of the Sentry say. "All the noise and fighting. We still caught the Rebel."

Whipping around, he saw that the Old Man had been taken captive. Two large and particularly cruel-looking members of the Sentry held him, arms pinned painfully behind his back. He appeared dazed, barely conscious. Blood smeared one side of his wrinkled face. His temper boiled thinking of what the Sentry must have done to him.

The Old Man saw him as well, but quickly looked away. Obviously, he didn't want the Sentry to know there was a connection between them.

It was all over then, he thought to himself. This new opportunity, this new hope, however small, was gone.

———

AFTER THE EXCITEMENT ended and the crowd cleared, two of the Sentry warned Daman to remain near his home should he be wanted during the trial. He did not argue with them. After his imprudent words, he fully expected to be hauled to the Keep himself. Apparently the Sentry decided to be generous, realizing he was young and under a great deal of stress. Xander's bluff about the "blow to his head" probably helped as well.

He went to the Keep. He was refused entrance. They would not let him visit his father.

On his way back, he met his mother. She had been at the grove near Blaine River collecting berries and had just heard what happened. She looked as if she had aged ten years since breakfast.

"Have you seen your father?" He knew she was fighting back tears.

"Not since he was taken away."

"They say he aided the Rebel. That he's part of this Resistance that fights the Sentinel."

"Yes," he said, bowing his head. "That is what they say."

"I do not believe it. It cannot be true."

"No, Mother," he whispered. "It is not true."

Her eyes burned down on him, splitting his soul.

She knew. He was sure of it. She knew he was the one who had betrayed the Sentinel. She knew it was his fault Father had been arrested and beaten. She knew it was his fault her husband would be executed, leaving her without a partner for the rest of her days, leaving her with no one but a disobedient son who would soon lose his Winnowing and be transported somewhere else.

Her face trembled, but she said nothing more. She brushed past him and entered the front office of the Keep. A few moments later, she too was turned away.

He sat on the steps outside, too unhappy for words. He had been foolish and impetuous, as always. He was the most miserable wretch that ever lived. And the worst son.

————

ABOUT HALF AN HOUR LATER, Daman saw Mykah emerge from the Keep. Mykah walked past without speaking. Then, as if by afterthought, he stopped.

"You must understand," he said quietly. "These are troubled times. This old Rebel and his Resistance—they pose a great threat to our way of life. The Sentinel must be protected."

He fought back the words that came to mind.

"The Captain of the Guard has decided not to prosecute you for your foolish words and actions," Mykah continued. "We all agreed that you were in a strained frame of mind and did not know what you were saying." He paused. "I personally assured them that you did not mean what you said."

His eyes rose. "I did mean it."

Mykah's mouth became thin and tight. "Daman, listen to me. We are no longer children, passing our time at games and nonsense. I'm a member of the Black Sentry. I must obey and enforce the Laws and Ways of the Sentinel."

"I will never obey the Sentinel."

"Then from this day forward, we can no longer be friends."

He stared at Mykah, barely able to believe his own ears. They had always been friends—*always*. As far back as he could remember.

"There's more." Mykah shifted uncomfortably from one foot to the other. "If I learn you're part of this Resistance, or you're acting contrary to the Laws and Ways of the Sentinel, I will report you to the Magistrate. Do you understand?"

He did not answer.

"Make no mistake, Daman. I *will* report you." He turned abruptly and walked away.

"Goodbye, friend," he whispered, long after Mykah was gone.

———

Daman sat on the stoop for a long while and thought as long and as hard as he had ever done before. He knew he was at a critical turning point. The decisions he made today would set the stage for the rest of his life—however long or short it might be.

He was responsible for all that had happened.

And since he was responsible, he decided at last, it was time he acted responsibly.

He walked to the headquarters of the Black Sentry, adjacent to the Arena. He went to the back entrance and pounded on the door.

The Sentry on duty peered out.

"Go away!" he shouted. "You've already been told. You may not see your father before trial."

"That is not why I came." He tried to keep his voice firm, although he was trembling inside.

"Then what?"

"I wish to speak to the Prosecutor."

"And what would you want with him? If this is some sort of game—"

"It's no game, sir. I have business with the Prosecutor."

"He's busy."

"Get him anyway."

"Don't tell me what to do, you—"

"I have come to give the Prosecutor information. Important information." He dropped his voice to a whisper. "Information about the Resistance."

The Sentry's head twitched. "How do I know you're not lying?"

"I'm not lying. And if you don't get the Prosecutor, I'll let it be known throughout the village that you prevented important information about the Resistance from reaching the Prosecutor. I do not think he will be pleased. Do you?"

He could see the man wanted to knock him off the step. But he couldn't risk incurring the Prosecutor's wrath. "One minute," he growled.

The man disappeared. He waited, his heart thumping wildly in his chest.

The Sentry returned with someone about Daman's father's age, the same man he had seen leading the assault on his home only hours before. His name was Arlen Crusher. He was the senior officer and Captain of the Guard, which entitled him to serve as Prosecutor. He was a tall man with black hair and small, dark eyes. He wore a solemn expression at all times— never the least hint of a smile.

His voice was slow and heavy. "I am told you have something you wish to tell me."

"You have taken my father on charges of harboring the Rebel."

"This is so."

"The Black Sentry has acted in error. My father committed no crime."

"You are a loyal son and you speak out of a well-placed affection. Unfortunately—"

"No, sir," he said emphatically. "I do not speak out of affection. I speak out of fact. I know my father did not commit this crime."

The Proseutor's left eyebrow arched. "And how do you know this?"

He drew in his breath. "Because I committed this crime. I was the one who hid the Rebel in our cellar. My father knew nothing about it. I'm the guilty one."

# FOURTEEN

Daman held his breath until the Prosecutor spoke.

"Do you know what you say, boy?"

"I do," he replied, maintaining a calm exterior that bore no resemblance to the turmoil he felt within.

"And you say it, nonetheless."

"Because it's the truth. I can prove it. I can provide details. Things no one else could know. Certainly not my father."

Crusher wasted no more time. He called for two more Sentry and had Daman escorted to a cell. He warned them to say nothing of what they had heard until they received further instruction.

The two Sentry, both men older than him but whom he'd known most of his life, hauled him to a cell in the Keep. Neither spoke a word.

He spent the night in a dark iron-barred room with no light except the scant moonlight that shone through a high barred window. There was a bare cot but no other furniture or comfort of any kind. He was not allowed to see anyone. All he could do was curl up on the cot and try to sleep.

When at last he did drift off, his dreams were haunted.

———

Morning came abruptly. Four guards marched into his cell while he still slept. They hauled him to his feet and dragged him through the door. He was given only a few moments to wash and prepare himself.

"What's going to happen?" he asked.

The Sentry sneered, but none would answer.

Eventually he was taken to a larger room he knew to be the Courtroom of the Black Sentry. He had been here with his father on a few occasions, when neighbors were tried for offenses against the Sentinel. Offenses for which they were always found guilty.

The courtroom gallery was packed with villagers. Every seat was filled.

Brita was there, but instead of sitting with her family, she sat beside Xander. What possible reason could Xander have for being here? After the incident with Lieutenant Coffin, he should be as far from the Prosecutor as possible. He wouldn't have been admitted to the courtroom unless a request was made by someone outside the slave class.

And why would Brita sit with him?

His father sat at the front, his face dark and bruised. Daman's mother sat behind him. They were surrounded by Black Sentry.

One person who was notably not present was the Old Man. Why would they not force him to attend a prosecution that was all about him?

The guards pushed his father into a chair on a raised platform, then stood behind him.

Prosecutor Crusher entered, the usual solemn expression on his face, frocked in his most formal ceremonial robe. He was followed by Benjamin Coffin and the village Magistrate. These three would decide his fate.

He spotted another person passing through the doorway. He eyes widened.

The Acolyte said not a word, but found a place in the center of the courtroom. He stood there silently, watching.

"The trial shall begin," Crusher pronounced. The crowd quieted. "The charge is that Daman Adkins, a boy of this village, has purposefully and intentionally conspired to commit treason with enemies of the Sentinel and furthermore has committed heresy against the Sentinel. This court shall consider the evidence and render judgment accordingly."

He was relieved to hear that his father was not listed as one of the accused.

Prosecutor Crusher stepped down from the raised platform and stood before him. According to the Laws and Ways of the Sentinel, he would be permitted no counsel, he would be forced to testify, and he would not be permitted to call witnesses on his own behalf. He could only defend himself to the extent he was able while answering the questions put to him.

The first witness called was a Lieutenant Howe in the Black Sentry platoon attached to another village called Sandego, far from Merrindale. His outfit had chased the Rebel for three days. According to Howe, the Rebel and several of his associates were involved in the theft of an important treasure. The associates were captured. Only the Rebel escaped.

No explanation or description of the device stolen was given —for good reason, he suspected. They did not want people to know anything about it. He could only conclude that the device stolen was the red-tinted key the Old Man had shown them in the cellar. He wondered how such a tiny object could cause so much concern.

Lieutenant Howe explained that, once they chased the

Rebel to the outskirts of Merrindale, he was joined by a new companion.

"Did you see this other person?" Crusher asked.

"Not clearly. But it was someone young. A boy."

He felt the eyes in the courtroom turning toward him, scrutinizing him.

"Could you describe the boy you saw? His height. His size."

"He had brown hair, cut just above his shoulders. Medium height. Slim but sturdy build."

"An exact description of the boy who now stands on trial, isn't it?"

He wanted to protest. That vague description could have described any number of boys in the village. But he was not allowed to speak, and none were permitted to speak for him.

"Yes," Lieutenant Howe answered. "He fits the description perfectly."

The Prosecutor smiled. "You may step down."

The next witness was Mykah. As he walked to the front of the courtroom, their eyes briefly met. He felt ashamed. Mykah undoubtedly knew his friend had lied to him, had prevented him from finding the Old Man in the cellar.

Mykah explained that he'd been sent out with all the other available Sentry to scour the village for the Rebel. They'd searched houses, alleys, and stores when Mykah remembered that the Adkins home had a storage cellar behind it.

"What happened when you brought your platoon to the cellar?"

"After announcing myself, I led the group down the steps. We found Daman Adkins and . . . a young girl."

"Who was this girl?"

"I do not know. I never saw her face."

Now Mykah was the one lying—to protect Brita.

"What were they doing?"

"They . . ." Mykah craned his neck awkwardly. "They appeared to be kissing."

Crusher waited for the stir in the courtroom to pass. "You thought they were engaged in an unauthorized display of affection?"

"I did, yes. And Daman told me he had not seen the Rebel."

"And because Daman Adkins was your friend, you left without searching the cellar."

"That's true, sir. I did."

Crusher folded his arms across his chest. "You realize now that Daman Adkins lied to you, don't you?"

"Yes."

"You realize that your friend—and probably this girl as well —were part of the Resistance, and that they intentionally misled you to prevent you from discovering the enemy of the Sentinel."

"I do."

"You allowed the Old Man to escape—however briefly— because you had feelings of friendship. But you must now see that ideas like friendship are of no value to the Black Sentry. That you must do the will of the Sentinel without regard for such trivialities. Don't you?"

"Yes," Mykah said firmly. "I do now."

Crusher nodded curtly. "You may step down."

He could not look at Mykah as he left the courtroom. He knew Mykah felt betrayed. He had endangered Mykah's career almost before it had begun. Even more than before, Daman felt that a stone wall fell between them, one never likely to be breached.

Crusher called another member of the Sentry. He was tall and athletic, but with a frightening countenance. His name was James Kent. He was the man who led the platoon that burst into their home and found the Old Man.

"What did you do when you spotted the Rebel?" the Prosecutor asked.

"At first we surrounded the house."

"And then?"

"The rear door was blocked, so we all came around to the front and eventually forced our way inside."

"Did you find the Rebel?"

"Apparently, he escaped through the rear while we struggled to enter the front."

"Why did you not pursue him?"

"We tried. But as we passed through the room, someone held us back, bombarding us with anything at hand."

"And who was this attacker?"

Kent pointed toward Daman's father. "The baker. Martin Adkins."

"Was he protecting the Old Man?"

"I thought so at first. But the Old Man had already departed. Mister Adkins later explained he did not know the Rebel hid in his home. I believe it was the boy who admitted the Rebel without his parents' knowledge or consent. I believe Mister Adkins panicked when he saw the Sentry burst through his door. He thought the Sentry had come for him."

"Regrettable," Crusher pronounced. "But understandable."

He felt a wave of relief flood through him. As long as they believed that—his father should be safe.

"Were you able to subdue Mister Adkins?"

"Of course. And a few moments later we captured the Old Man as well."

"You may step down. And now," the Prosecutor said, "there remains to be called but a single witness."

The prosecutor turned suddenly and glared down at him. "And that witness, young Master Adkins, is you."

# FIFTEEN

Daman steeled himself as he sat in the witness chair. He knew the questioning would be relentless. He had to remain strong.

"We have many questions for you," Crusher said. "You will tell us everything."

He looked away from the crowd, trying to block those penetrating eyes out of his mind.

"I have already told you everything, sir," he replied.

"You will address me as Prosecutor, boy."

There was a slight stirring. "Actually," the Acolyte said, in a tranquil, serene voice, "I believe I should act as Prosecutor from this point forward."

Crusher was obviously surprised. "You?"

The Acolyte spread wide his hands. "Of course. It is my right, as senior representative of the Sentinel. If you have an objection—"

"No, no," Crusher said hastily. "Of course not." As surprised as he might be, he knew better than to challenge the Acolyte's authority. "Do you wish me to continue the interrogation?"

"Of course," the Acolyte said generously. "Please do. Although I may interrupt from time to time."

Crusher bowed his head obediently, then returned his attention to his witness. "You will tell us everything you know about the Rebel you sheltered in your cellar."

He had already decided that, so far as was possible without endangering others, he would tell the truth. This seemed the best plan, because he worried that if he were caught up in a web of falsehoods, they might disbelieve him and once again accuse his father. Therefore, he gave them a reasonably truthful account of meeting the Old Man and running from the Black Sentry. He omitted the encounter with the Creeper and everything he had learned about the hideous beasts, instead suggesting that they'd had the good fortune not to encounter any.

"You must live a charmed life," Crusher said. "In the generations since the protective fences were erected, few have ever ventured into the Creepers' forest and lived to tell of it."

"I've always been lucky," he said, and left it at that. But he noticed that the Acolyte peered at him most intently.

"Why did you help this Rebel when he appeared unexpectedly?" Crusher asked.

"I don't know. There was little time to think."

"Do you harbor enmity toward the Sentinel?"

"Then or now?"

The gallery stirred.

"Then."

"I was not aware of any enmity. I simply saw a man being hunted like an animal and tried to help him."

"And now?"

"Now I have seen my father hurt and humiliated by the Sentinel and his minions even though he is guilty of no crime. I can no longer in good conscience say that the Laws and Ways of the Sentinel are infallible because I have seen that they are not."

A stunned silence fell over the courtroom. Words such as his had never been heard in this village, certainly not in any public proceeding. Several of the men in the gallery shouted for an immediate Ritual of Execution.

But he noted that some of the others sat quietly, as if perhaps his words had affected them in quite a different way.

He glanced at his parents. His mother pressed one hand against her forehead. He supposed she was horrified by his words, and frightened by what she knew would be the inevitable result. His father's expression was also grave, but he did not perceive any hint of shame. Perhaps he imagined it, but for a moment he thought perhaps his father even felt some pride that he had the courage to speak the truth.

"Tell us what happened next," Crusher prodded.

He told them about returning to the village after night fell, eluding the Sentry, and making his way to the cellar. Of course, he omitted any mention of Brita.

"You knew that the man you harbored was the Rebel the Acolyte had warned about, did you not?"

"I didn't *know* it," he answered truthfully.

"You suspected it was so."

"Yes."

"Nonetheless, you gave him aid and succor."

"I gave him a place to sleep and food to eat."

"And you made no report to the officials."

"Why would I? I'd never seen him do anything wrong. He committed no crime against me."

Crusher whipped back his hand and slapped him across the face. The blow stung. He felt water surging to his eyes. "Don't play games with me, boy. You saw him being chased by the Black Sentry. You knew he was wanted."

He made no reply. Crusher's words spoke for themselves.

"The Sentry reported seeing a young girl in your cellar that night who helped you dissuade the Sentry from searching. Is that true?"

"It is."

"And who was this girl?"

He hesitated.

"Was it a girl from the village?"

"No," he answered. "Another stranger."

"A member of this Resistance?"

"Yes." Why not let them believe the Resistance was endless and everywhere?

"Are there more of these Rebels?"

"More than you know," he answered quietly. "More than you can imagine."

There was an audible rumble from the gallery.

"Are you now or have you ever been a member of the Resistance?"

"No," he answered.

"Then answer this," said the Acolyte, raising his voice, "if you had the chance to join this Resistance, would you?"

He thought a long time before answering. "I don't know."

"Did you tell your parents what you'd done?"

"Never," he said firmly. He had to make them believe it. "I told them nothing. Because I knew that if I did, they would not approve, and they would make an immediate report to the Black Sentry, as required by the Laws and Ways."

"And yet, you gave the Old Man food—"

"I stole it. My parents did not know. They have always respected the Sentinel's Laws."

"Let me ask you another question. Do you feel any shame for having betrayed the Sentinel? Do you feel any remorse?"

"I'm sorry my actions caused harm to my father. And my mother."

"But the Sentinel, boy. What about the Sentinel?"

He knew what the smartest answer to this question would be, but somehow he found himself saying something altogether different. He had an opportunity to do more, an opportunity he shouldn't—*couldn't*—let pass. "The Sentinel is a cruel master who forces people to do his bidding without regard for their own needs or well-being."

The roar from the gallery was loud, but Crusher managed to make his voice even louder. "Then you are an enemy of the Sentinel," he bellowed, pointing a finger. "You hope to destroy him."

"I have never made any plans against the Sentinel, nor wanted to. But if I could find a way to restore freedom to the people of Merrindale, I would."

"Meaning you would destroy our orderly society."

"There can be no freedom so long as the Sentinel dictates every aspect of our lives." He turned toward the gallery. "We do not have to live like this!"

Crusher grabbed him and shoved him back into his seat. Everyone in the courtroom tried to speak at once. The proceeding became chaotic until the Acolyte cut in, silencing Crusher and the crowd with a single gesture. "The evidence is clear. This examination is concluded."

Crusher tried to protest. "But I still—"

The Acolyte's eyes blazed.

Crusher stepped back to the raised platform and retook his seat. "The examination is concluded."

"And I assume there are no other witnesses," the Acolyte said.

Crusher shook his head. "I see no need. What more proof

could you want? What more could any court want? The boy's guilt is clear. You have confessed it yourself, Daman Adkins."

"That is not true. I wish to speak on my own behalf."

The Acolyte did not even look at him. "Denied."

"But surely I have the right—"

"Silence." Again, the Acolyte made the slashing gesture that brought immediate quiet. "You have said quite enough. You are not to speak another word. If he tries to do so, I instruct the Sentry to gag him."

As the panel decided his fate, he stared out into the crowd. For the first time, he found some eyes willing to meet his. Was the Acolyte so afraid of his words that he could not even be permitted to speak?

The Acolyte spoke again. "Rise, Martin Adkins."

He felt a clutching at his heart. What did the Acolyte want with his father?

"It is the decided opinion of this panel, having considered all the evidence put before us, that you have committed no crime and thus have not been charged. You still bear some responsibility in this matter. You may be guilty of failing to properly instruct your son to obey the Laws and Ways of the Sentinel. But we find no evidence that you intentionally committed any act of treason. Therefore, you and your wife are free to go."

His mother wrapped her arms around his father, a display of affection such as he had never witnessed between them before. Relief swept through his own heart as well.

"Daman Adkins, you will rise."

He pushed himself to his feet. His knees trembled. He hoped he did not look as frightened as he felt.

"While your father may have acted without malice toward the Sentinel, and may at best be guilty of negligent disregard, you are quite a different matter. Despite being not yet sixteen years of age, you hold great hatred and disrespect for the Laws and Ways of the Sentinel. You have no sense of right and wrong, and you deliberately and with malice aforethought took actions that you knew aided the enemies of the Sentinel. It is apparent to this panel that you are a young man with no conscience, a young man capable of unspeakable offenses against our orderly way of life."

The courtroom was deathly quiet. "You cannot be allowed to live in consort with civilized men. You are a contaminating influence, a danger to the peace of the village. Therefore, despite your young age, you must receive the maximum sentence. The Ritual of Execution."

A gasp went up—from his mother. Everyone else knew this verdict was inevitable. Perhaps she did, too, but tried to tell herself otherwise.

"Tonight," the Acolyte continued, "there will be a ceremony of worship and rededication in the Arena. Let all those who are loyal to the Sentinel come and prove it with reverence and charity. We will know who our friends are—and by their omission, our enemies."

The Black Sentry guarding him clamped their hands down on his shoulders. Without waiting for him to rise, they jerked him out of the witness chair and hauled him through the courtroom. None of the villagers spoke as he passed through the gallery. His father acted as if he wanted to, but he never had a chance.

The last sight he had was of his mother, her face buried in wet hands.

# SIXTEEN

They dragged Daman back to the Keep, then locked him in the same miserable cell as before.

He slumped down on the cot. How had he managed to destroy his life so utterly in only a few days? So many questions raced through his brain. He had no answers for any of them. And given the bleak prospects for his future, he was never likely to.

He heard footsteps outside the cell—slow, shuffling boots on the stone floor. He peered through the bars. The uniform told him it was Black Sentry. A guard posted to make sure he stayed put until sunrise.

Only when the boots came close to the bars could he identify the guard—Mykah.

This couldn't be a coincidence. The Captain of the Guard must have posted Mykah here intentionally, perhaps as a loyalty test. Or perhaps Mykah requested the assignment, to prove he had buried all feelings of friendship.

"I want a word with you," Mykah said.

"Have you come to lecture me again on my duty to the Sentinel?"

"No. I've come to try to talk some sense into you. Whatever you may think, Daman, I haven't forgotten that we were once friends. I still care what happens to you. So please—call for the Prosecutor. Repent. Beg for mercy. It's still possible your sentence could be commuted."

He knew Mykah was trying to help, but he also knew that would never happen. "No."

"Please. If not for yourself—do it for your family."

"I'm sorry. No."

"The Old Man has already been transported out of the village."

His chin rose.

"He's being sent to the village of Clovis. His Ritual of Execution will be the principal feature of their Spring Festival, which takes place tomorrow. I shouldn't be surprised if your Ritual was granted the same . . . honor." He drew in his breath. "Please, Daman. While there's still time. Repent."

"I'm sorry. I won't."

Mykah stiffened. "Then I can't help you." He turned, glancing toward the door. "You have a visitor."

He was surprised he was allowed visitors. He was even more surprised when he identified the man who walked quickly toward his cell.

"Father!" He stretched his arms through the bars of his cell. "I'm so sorry!"

"There is no need, son," his father replied quietly.

"How did you persuade the Sentry to let you in?"

"I've lived in this village many years, Daman. I have many friends—even in the Black Sentry."

"Father," he started, and all at once the words tumbled out. "I know I've shamed you. I don't know what happened—"

His father pressed close to the cell bars. "You're wrong You haven't shamed anyone."

"I have. I saw the expression on Mother's face—"

"Listen to me." He glanced over his shoulder, making sure no one was close enough to listen. "Someone has to fight the Sentinel's tyranny. Someone has to stand against him and his minions." He paused. "And it should have been me, not you. I'm the one who should be ashamed."

Daman's lips parted. He didn't know what to say.

"All my life I've hated the Sentinel, hated everything about his heartless, bland . . . orderly world. But I didn't have the courage to resist. In my entire life, I never had a tenth of the courage you displayed today in that courtroom."

"It would've been smarter to keep my mouth shut."

"Perhaps. But your words needed to be said. Surely you noticed how some of the people in the gallery reacted. Many in that room agreed with you, even if they were not able to say so. We need leaders, men and women willing to speak the truth and speak it loud. You've started a fire burning, Daman. If others join the cause, if others are willing to be as brave as you were today, then the Sentinel might yet be defeated."

"I don't know why I did it," he said quietly. "I just . . . knew it was the right thing to do." He paused. "There's one thing I don't understand, though. I left the Old Man in the cellar. How did he get inside the house?"

"I brought him in."

"But—how did you know he was in the cellar?"

A smile flashed across his father's face. "I knew it the instant I looked into your eyes. You're a poor liar."

"But—"

"He's an old friend of mine, as it turns out, from when I was a boy, before I reached the age of Winnowing. A friend of mine —and Abigail's. We were having a very pleasant chat—until the Black Sentry discovered us."

"That's my fault. Bringing him home was a mistake."

"Nonsense. What else could you do? But you did make one mistake. You should have let me take the blame."

"Never."

"What does it matter if they take me? I'm old—only a few years from my journey to Balaveria. You're young. You have your whole life ahead. And this village—this world—needs you. Someone to lead the fight against the Sentinel."

"But Father . . . you said—"

"Never mind what I said before. Listen to me now." He reached through the bars and squeezed his son's arm tightly. "Don't make the mistakes I did. Be true to your heart. Do what you know is right."

He looked back into his eyes and nodded. "Yes, Father. I will."

"But first, we have to get you out of here. Otherwise you won't be leading anyone anywhere."

"Mykah stands guard," he whispered.

"Yes, and there are other guards outside. It will not be easy. But I will see what I can do."

"But—how could you possibly—"

His father winked. "This old baker still knows a few tricks." He glanced once more over his shoulder. "It may well be that— well—" He hesitated. "I don't know if we will see one another again, so I'd best say this now." A warm smile crossed his face. "I'm very proud of you, Daman. Never give up." He squeezed his hands tightly. "Godspeed, son."

After his father left, he stood on tiptoes under the high barred window, trying to get an outside view, but he was not tall enough to look out. He felt as if he had been separated from the entire world. He could sense it, and he knew it was there. But he could take no part in it. Perhaps he never would again.

Still, it comforted him to hear the sounds. The clackety-clack of cart wheels on cobblestones, the opening and shutting of doors, the animals baying in the night. He pulled his cot close to the window and lay down on it, listening to the familiar sounds that would soon be lost to him forever, until at last he fell asleep.

———

DAMAN WAS AWAKENED by a stinging sensation in his eyes. He reached up as if to brush something away, but there was nothing there. He inhaled deeply—and gagged.

He sat upright. He tried to shout out, but his voice caught and he was overcome with coughing.

His eyes and nose burned. In the moonlight that crept into the cell, he spotted dark billowing clouds.

Smoke. But how—?

He felt a burning sensation on his leg. He looked down, coughing fitfully, straining to see through blurred eyes.

His cot was on fire.

# SEVENTEEN

Daman leaped off the cot, but not in time. The leg of his trousers caught the flame.

He tried to beat it down with his hands, but it was too hot and too fast. The flames began to burn.

Desperately, he whipped off his tunic and used it to squelch the fire. A few seconds later, it was still smoking, but extinguished. He tore the bottom part of his pant leg off so it wouldn't singe his leg. Then he whipped the flames on the mattress.

Too much time had passed. The blaze engulfed half the cot. The thick smoke cloud billowing up and the red-hot heat emanating from the cot made it impossible to stand close.

He ran to the bars of his cell.

"Mykah!" he cried, but his words were choked down by coughing. He covered his mouth, inhaled carefully, and tried again. "Mykah!"

He heard a door creak open, then footsteps. "What have you done?" Mykah shouted.

"Nothing."

"Is this some sort of trick?"

"Trick? I nearly burned to death in my sleep." He was barely able to get the last words out. The cot was entirely incinerated. Only a huge bright bonfire burned where it once had been. The cloud of smoke was so thick and suffocating he could barely breathe. "Please help me."

"I can't let you out. I have my instructions."

"Please!" His voice was hoarse and gravelly. He began to feel lightheaded. "I'll die in here."

Mykah bit down on his lower lip, then turned away.

"Mykah! Please!"

A moment later, Mykah faced the wall at the end of the corridor. He laid his hand on one of the stones. The stone gave way. There was a tiny recess behind. Mykah reached in—and came back with the key to the cell.

Mykah raced to the cell and inserted the key into the lock. The door swung open. He raced out, choking and gasping for air.

"Thank you, Mykah," he said, as soon as he could catch his breath. "Thank you for—"

To his astonishment, he saw Mykah's eyes roll closed, his knees crumble, and his body fall to the floor.

"Mykah?" Hidden in the smoke and shadows, a shimmering form emerged.

Xander.

How had he gotten in here? What was he doing? What happened to Mykah? His mind reeled, and to make his confusion even worse, he suddenly realized there was a second figure in the shadows.

Brita.

They both wore dark cloaks with hoods over their heads, ceremonial robes of the sort that many people wore to the various festivals and celebrations of the Sentinel. But why was Brita staring at him?

Suddenly embarrassed, he slipped his tunic back on. Xander lifted his right arm. He held a thick wooden club.

Brita reached under her cloak and withdrew a backpack. Reaching inside, she pulled out a length of strong rope. Xander took his knife and cut two pieces perhaps a foot and a half in length. Then she put the remainder of the rope back in the pack.

"What are you doing?"

"What does it look like? We're helping you escape, you fool!"

He bristled. "I didn't ask for your help."

"Of course not. You probably thought turning yourself in was a brilliant plan."

"Why did you involve Xander?"

"Xander volunteered. And I needed help."

Xander volunteered? To risk his neck? Why would a slave do such a thing? "How did you get in here?"

"By a combination of deception and brute force. I provided the deception. Xander provided the brute force."

"But the guards—"

"Your father distracted a few long enough for us to sneak inside the Keep."

"He's part of this?"

"Of course. Who did you think threw the charred ember through your cell window after we sneaked inside? Fortunately, most of the Sentry are at the Arena. Most everyone is, thanks to the Acolyte suggesting that anyone who did not attend would be judged a traitor. Xander only had to club a few guards to get to your cell."

His brain struggled to catch up. "You set my cot on fire on purpose."

"You don't miss a trick, do you?" Brita and Xander tied

Mykah to the bars of the cell. The fire, having nothing more to feed it, was dying out.

"Why not just club Mykah like the others?"

"Because we didn't know where he kept the key to your cell, idiot. We had to trick him into getting the key before I could let Xander brain him."

It was a clever deception, he had to admit. "How did you think of such a devious plan?"

"I read it in a book."

"Well, I should . . . thank you. Your plan was good."

"My plan was flawless," she corrected.

He tilted his head to one side. "I did burn my leg a bit . . ."

"Don't whine. We got you out, didn't we?"

"Yes. But you might've warned me."

"Your father tried. You were sound asleep and your guard would have heard him had he spoken loud enough to be heard over your snoring."

"I do not snore."

"You do. But we have more important matters to discuss. We must get out of here as soon as possible. The Sentry will soon realize you've escaped." She tossed him a dark cloak like the ones they both wore. "Put this on."

He followed her directions. She grabbed his arm and pulled him toward the exit.

They moved at a quiet but brisk pace, careful not to attract any unnecessary attention.

He spotted another Black Sentry guard lying unconscious and tied fast. He showed no signs of stirring any time soon.

Xander led the way through the confusing maze of corridors that led to the outer office of the Keep. Apparently he had been sent on errands here in the past and had some familiarity with the layout. They were almost at the outer door when he heard an earsplitting noise.

"The alarm bell," Brita muttered.

"But who—?"

"I don't know," she replied. "But someone knows you're free. In a few moments, every Black Sentry platoon in the village will be here. *Run.*"

CHAPTER

# EIGHTEEN

Daman and his two companions bolted out of the Keep, moving as fast as their legs would carry them, Xander leading the way. Fortunately, the loose-fitting black cloaks did not restrict their movements.

Xander was the fastest runner in the group. Brita had obviously spent more time with books than at the Summer Games. Nonetheless, she managed to keep pace. Her feet moved as quickly as his and at times threatened to surpass him.

When they entered the main crossroads of the village, someone spotted them.

"Look!" a man cried out, pointing. "It's Adkins. He's escaped!"

After a moment's confusion, a clamor arose. He knew it wouldn't be long before someone came after them. And the Black Sentry could not be far behind.

They could see the North Gate, which of course was not open.

He looked at Brita. "Where do we go now?"

"Outside."

"With the Creepers? The Savages?"

"Why not? You did."

"With the Old Man, yes. But not for long. And not alone."

"You aren't alone." She ran to the tall fence adjoining the Gate and stopped. "You have me to protect you."

Brita pulled another length of rope out of her backpack. One end was tied to a large iron hook, much like the one the Old Man used. Xander slung it up to the top of the fence. It caught on the first attempt.

They shinnied up the rope, him first, emulating how he had seen the Old Man do it. Xander and Brita followed.

And then he looked down the opposite side of the fence.

Creepers.

On the ground below he saw not one but three Creepers moving rapidly toward the fence. He shivered as he watched their now all too familiar, grotesque, quivering approach. They moved back and forth along the wall, whirling their tentacles in the air, searching for a way up. He knew that if he or the others so much as set foot on the ground, they would be killed.

Back in the village, he saw a Sentry platoon fast approaching.

Creepers before and Sentry behind. They were trapped—with nowhere to go.

"Xander," he asked, "can you hook the rope onto a branch on the nearest tree?"

Xander immediately understood what he had in mind. "I can try."

Xander swung the hook in the air, then let it fly. Once again, he got it on the first try. The hook locked down on an upper branch.

"You go first. Swing over, then throw the rope back to us."

Xander didn't argue. He held tight to the rope, pushed off, and swung into the nearest tree, sailing over the heads—and deadly tails—of the Creepers.

After he was secure, Xander threw the rope back to the others. The Sentry were scant moments away.

"Come on," he told Brita. "You're next."

She looked at him, horrified, but didn't move. Brita had not been introduced to the Creepers before as he had. She was transfixed by the horrific, gelatinous monsters and their black slimy trail—just as he had been, the first time he saw them. She had been taught her whole life that coming close to a Creeper would mean instant death. And she did not want to die.

"We don't have time to argue," he said. "Come on."

"I'm sorry, Daman—I—I can't."

"You have to."

"I *can't!*"

"I'll help you."

"No—I—I just—"

"Brita." The lead Sentry was so close now he could make out the man's face. It was Crusher, the Captain of the Guard. "Brita, the Old Man is counting on you. You're his last hope."

Those were the words that made the difference. In spite of her fear, Brita gritted her teeth and grabbed the rope.

"Don't do it!" Crusher cried, only a few feet from the fence. "It's suicide. You'll be killed."

There wasn't enough time for them to cross separately. "Put your arms around my neck," he instructed Brita.

He could see she was still terrified, but she did it. An instant later, he pushed away from the fence.

Together, they swung through the air into the forest. The wind rushed across their faces, sending a chill of excitement through his bones. He saw the Creepers beneath them, reacting in frustration and displeasure as their prey sailed away. At last they grabbed the nearest branches of the tree.

Although he could no longer see them, he could hear the consternation on the other side of the fence. A handful of Sentry argued, trying to persuade someone to follow the escapees into the forest. No one volunteered. Even the harshest commands could not change their minds. Although the Sentry did occasionally travel outside the village, it was always by daylight, always in large groups, and usually in the relative safety of a cart or wagon drawn by horse or livestock. No one wanted to plunge out there in the dark on foot.

Three Creepers pounded against the fence.

"That's an order!" he heard one of the leaders shout.

"But they'll kill me!"

"If the traitors can do it, so can you."

"I do not wish to die."

And so it went. It would take some time before Crusher could persuade someone to follow them into the forest. They had time—a little anyway.

He and Brita were secure on their branch, just below Xander. Brita clung tightly to his arm.

"We must move on immediately," he whispered.

"Why?" Xander asked. "You don't think the Creepers can climb trees, do you?"

"I know they can." He pointed. Below them, three Creepers circled, whirling their long tails toward a low branch. "We must move."

Fortunately, the trees were tightly packed in this part of the forest, so they were able to continue making their way as before. Xander would either jump or swing to the next tree, then he and Brita would follow. In this manner, they managed to stay one step ahead of the Creepers.

At one point, he saw Brita staring down at the malevolent creatures, repulsed, yet unable to take her eyes off them. "They're hideous," she whispered.

"What did you expect?"

"I never knew. They aren't in any of my books. My mother

sometimes suggested that the Creepers were a fantasy, a myth invented by the Sentinel to keep villagers where he wanted them. I see now that isn't true."

"No. The Creepers are real. And very deadly."

Eventually, they outdistanced the Creepers. Slowly, cautiously, once they were sure it was safe, they made their descent, watching at all times for more of the hideous beasts. Fortunately, the moon was full and bright. They were able to see clearly, even deep into the forest.

After a while, they removed their cloaks. Brita stored them in her pack.

"It seems we have escaped," Xander said, surveying the strange new world around him.

"Yes," he echoed. "But where are we?"

He had no idea. How could they find their way to safety?

Discounting his minor excursion two days before, they were outside the village for the first time in their entire lives.

And they were lost. And they were alone.

# PART TWO

THE JOURNEY

CHAPTER

# NINETEEN

"We must all remain quiet," Daman said. "At the first sound of a Creeper, make for the nearest tree."

"Understood," Xander replied. "What I don't understand is where we're going. And how we'll get there."

"We should go to Clovis. That's the nearest village. And that's where they've taken the Old Man."

"Can you get us there, Daman?"

He thought a moment. "I saw the map, briefly, but—"

"It's a lucky thing you have me along." Brita swung her pack off her back and reached inside. A moment later, she retrieved a tiny, glittering red object.

"The Key! Where did you find it?"

"Where you left it," she replied curtly. "After they took the Old Man, I slipped inside the cellar. If I hadn't, the Sentry would surely have found it eventually."

He peered into her pack. She was well prepared for this journey. She had a canteen, some dried meats and bread, a rind of cheese and a change of clothes. And one other item from the cellar he recognized.

"You brought the Map. This is wonderful." He removed the ribbon and unrolled it. "When you can read a map, there's no need to ever be lost."

"So I've read," she replied. "Unfortunately, I can't understand it."

"I can." His eyes twinkled. "Is it possible I could teach you something?"

"Seems unlikely." She frowned, then knelt beside him. "Show me how it's done."

———

WHILE THE SUN ROSE, Daman told Brita everything the Old Man taught him about reading maps. After they found the blue circle that represented Merrindale, they traced their route in the direction they believed they had come. By noting the position of the sun, they were able to determine which way they must walk to find the road to Clovis.

"What a wonderful invention this map is," Brita marveled.

He rolled it up and tucked it back into her pack. "Let's go."

They followed a trail through the forest. He noticed that Brita frequently stopped to touch things as she walked—the grass, the trees, the plant life.

"These trees are so different from those in the village," she remarked.

"Because they're real," he said, displaying the sage wisdom he had acquired the two days before from the Old Man.

"Then what are ours?"

"Fake. Manmade. Orderly."

"These seem so coarse. So irregular. But in a way—more interesting. More exciting."

He had to agree. Soon she pointed out the differences in the consistency of the grass, the wide variety of plants, the fact that the greenery grew randomly, rather than following an orderly pattern.

The three made their way through the dark forest. It seemed as if each step brought a new discovery. Some of what they saw seemed familiar—and yet still strangely different.

After they had walked for what seemed an eternity, he heard Xander shout: "Over here!"

Brita and Daman raced to catch up to him. There was a wide clearing in the forest, a dirt path dividing the trees into two sections.

"This must be the main road," Brita said, thinking aloud. She withdrew the map once again, checking their position. "We're about two miles north of Merrindale. If we stay on this road, we'll eventually arrive at Clovis."

"Assuming you're reading the map correctly," he added.

"Which I am." She folded the map and started down the road.

After a while, he noticed that the path under their feet had become harder. The road was no longer made of dirt, but of something more like rock—but not rock.

"It's paved," Brita explained.

"What does that mean?"

"It means . . . I'm not sure exactly. It's something the Ancients did. To make their roads stronger."

"Why?"

"The Ancients had vehicles far different from ours. Wonderful Constructs that moved without livestock to pull them."

"And . . . these Constructs required harder roads?"

"Yes. And wider ones. The Ancients took their Constructs everywhere."

He peered at the road beneath their feet. "This path seems

cracked and irregular. The grass has overgrown it in many places."

"It has been many years since the time of the Ancients. No one has cared for the road since the rise of the Sentinel. Nature quickly reclaims its own."

"Nature?" Again he was puzzled. He did not know the word.

She tried to explain. "Nature is . . . everything. Everything real. Everything that wasn't made by man or the Sentinel."

"Then where did it come from?"

She didn't answer. Instead, she raced forward. "Look!"

He followed close behind. They approached a small stream, about as wide across as an adult man is tall. But the road did not stop at the edge of the water. To his amazement, the road stretched across the top.

"What is it?" he asked.

"A bridge," she answered. "At least, I think it is. I've seen pictures. The Ancients used them to cross water without getting themselves—or their Constructs—wet."

"Is it safe?"

"Only one way to find out." Before he could protest, she raced across. An instant later, she stood on the other side.

He and Xander followed close behind. The bridge held his feet firmly, even though it did not touch the ground.

What marvels these Ancients had.

After walking another hour or so, they came to a large expanse of land riddled with hard rock, much like the material Brita had called the paved road. Here, though, broken pieces of the rock were not just on the road but everywhere. Rubble covered the grass and was strewn through the trees.

"This must've been an enormous road," he said.

"This was more than a road," she replied. "This was some kind of settlement. A town, perhaps."

"A town? Why would they pave a town?"

"The Ancients paved everything. They cut the trees and covered the grass. They poured their rock everywhere. Even their houses and meeting places were built upon it."

"Not much of it has survived."

"No. The Sentinel destroyed almost everything."

"Look! Both of you!"

Xander had dug something out of the ground, something half-buried beneath the rubble and debris. An arc-shaped piece of metal with soft round spongy material at both ends. A thick gray string dangled from one side.

"What is it?"

Brita didn't immediately answer. She took the device and held it one way, then the other.

"Surely you read something about this in one of your books? The ones that contain so much knowledge?"

"I'm sure I did," she hedged. "It's difficult to remember everything at once."

"It looks as if it might fit over your head," Daman suggested.

"You could be right." She slid the arc over her head. It fit loosely, but through trial and error she learned that she could manipulate the size of the arc by pushing in on the metal until it fit her head perfectly.

"The two spongy pieces fit right over my ears," she observed. "That can't be a coincidence."

"Perhaps it somehow spoke to the Ancients," Xander suggested.

"How could it speak?" she scoffed. "It's just metal and wire." She snapped her fingers. "Of course. It's a medical device. For the treatment of ears."

"Treatment of ears?"

"Exactly. I don't recall the name, but the soft parts are placed on the ends for the protection. Then the sponge could be pressed in to painlessly clean out the wax."

He squinted. "This is an ear-cleaner?"

"Yes. That's it. I'm certain." She picked up the gray cord. "And this could be inserted into some kind of power device. An engine of sorts. Then the device would send out healing energy."

"Are you sure about this?"

"Have you ever read a book?" she shot back.

"Well . . . no."

She yanked the device off her head. "Then you'll just have to take my word for it."

————

Toward the end of the day, Daman spotted a wooden structure off the side of the road. Brita suggested that it was an old barn. They crossed over to it, hoping to find someplace comfortable where they could catch some sleep.

Inside, they found enough hay and grass to make pallets on the floor. There were a few odd bits of furniture—a battered desk, some sort of feeding trough—but little else. They pulled enough together to create some rudimentary comforts. Brita withdrew two candles from her backpack and lit them, casting an orange glow over the interior of the barn.

"Look at this!" Brita said. In a pile of hay, she found a flat, white, oval-shaped frame.

"What is it?" he asked, peering over her shoulder.

She ran her hand over the smooth surface. "It's a Relic. From the Ancients."

"But what is it? What did it do?" He stared at her. "You don't know, do you?"

"Of course I do." She held it out in front of her. "It's a fire-box. For small cooking fires. The white frame keeps the fire from escaping." She placed it carefully on a patch of dirt. "Xander, do you have the flint?"

He nodded, then set to work sparking the fire. Brita removed some of the meat from her backpack.

They had almost settled in when he heard something.

The three of them sat upright. No one said anything.

The place was filled with hay and dust and cobwebs. A person—or anything else—could be hiding almost anywhere.

"It was probably nothing," he said, unconvincingly. He told himself it must have been his imagination.

He had settled back into his pallet and almost relaxed when he heard the sound again. This time, he was almost certain the noise came from above them.

There could be no question about it now.

They were not alone.

# TWENTY

Daman looked upward. The barn—or whatever it was —had an upper loft on the south end, high above their heads. It too was covered with hay. But in the far back, he thought he saw some of the hay . . . moving.

"We should leave," Xander said.

Brita agreed. "What if it's a Creeper?"

Daman peered up at the loft. "I don't think so."

A wooden ladder was nailed to the side wall. He took a loaf of bread Brita had laid out, then started up the ladder.

He reached the top, then took a few cautious steps forward. "Is anyone there?"

Something stirred. Something at the other end, in a great pile of hay.

He laid the bread down in front of him. "Are you hungry?"

The haystack vibrated, but no one emerged.

"There's plenty. And downstairs, we have cheese. I love cheese. Mmm. Yum."

The haystack trembled. Yellow straw tumbled from the top.

A head poked through the middle.

It was a man. His face was dirty, and his shirt was torn.

"It's all right. We won't hurt you."

The man slowly emerged from the haystack.

He was not of the village. He was dressed in rags, and his face showed signs of prolonged exposure to the sun.

He took a few steps out of the haystack, then crouched down and scampered across the loft. He didn't stop until they were almost nose to nose.

"Is the coast clear?" he whispered.

"I believe it to be, yes."

His face twitched one way, then the other. "You can never be sure. They have spies everywhere."

"Spies?"

His eyes rolled around full circle. "The hills have eyes."

"They do?"

"Of course they do. And the walls have ears."

"I . . . see."

"And I have a mouth. Are you planning to eat that bread?"

He handed the stranger the loaf. The man chewed it down ravenously.

He started down the loft. The stranger followed warily behind him. The old wooden steps were not nearly as secure as they must have been in the time of the Ancients, but they were sufficient to bear their weight. All four gathered around the small fire, where Brita warmed some of her cured meats, then passed them around.

He was surprised to find how hungry he was. Something about a jailbreak, not to mention an aerial flight through Creeper country, worked up an appetite.

Throughout the meal, the stranger's eyes darted all around the barn, always alert for any sign of activity. Finally the man spoke. "May I ask you a question?"

"Of course," Brita said. "What do you want to know?"

"Why are you cooking in a toilet seat?"

Brita appeared mortified.

He didn't entirely understand. "What do you mean?"

The stranger shook his head. "Never mind. My name is Drake. John Drake."

The three travelers greeted him.

"Are you from Clovis?" Brita asked.

Drake looked at her suspiciously. "Why would you ask that?"

"I . . . just wondered. It's not far . . ."

"No," he said. "I'm not from Clovis. Nice village, though."

"Then where are you from?"

"You ask a lot of questions, girl."

She drew up her chin. "Smart people always do. That's how we get smarter."

A tiny smile cracked on Drake's face. "You know . . . that's exactly right. That's the Method." He returned his attention to his food. "I'm not from anywhere."

"Does that mean you're an exile?"

"You . . . could say that. Yes. Fine. I'm an exile."

He had never met an exile before, or even thought it possible. He had always been taught that anyone separated from the village and the Sentinel would die within days. But the Old Man survived. And now it appeared this man did as well. "How long have you been an exile?"

"All my life."

"What?"

"My adult life, anyway. I did not submit to the Winnowing. I ran."

"But—it isn't possible."

Drake winked, then returned to his food. "Evidently it is."

Xander leaned forward cautiously. "Are you in the Sentry?"

Drake laughed. "Do I look like one? No, I'm an inventor."

He blinked. An inventor? Wasn't that what his father dreamed of being?

"But—how do you get around? How did you get here? Without being caught by the Creepers or the Savages?"

"No one ever spots me," Drake said mysteriously. "I'm lighter than air. I leave no tracks. I'm like the wind. *Whoosh!*" His hand glided toward them. "Fast and invisible." After another sibilant whoosh, the hand returned to earth.

"Why are you here? What are you doing?"

"I'm afraid I'm not at liberty to answer that question. Why have you three come here?"

They all looked at one another. Could they trust him? If he truly was an exile, then he might be sympathetic. But it seemed a terrible risk . . .

He coughed into his hand. "We've . . . uh . . . had a disagreement with the Black Sentry. And now . . . they're looking for us."

"Why do they want you?"

He hesitated, weighing the pros and cons of telling this strange man the truth. It would be safer to remain silent.

But he didn't. "I just escaped from a Black Sentry Keep."

Drake peered back at him. "Truly?"

He nodded. "But they are far behind us. They have no idea where we are now."

Drake resumed devouring the food. "I have had many unpleasant experiences at the hands of the Black Sentry."

"I can imagine."

"And it will only become worse. There are rumors in the air. The Sentinel is about to unleash a new kind of Sentry, a policing force greater than any he has used before. A force that will make him invincible."

Xander's expression was grim. "I have heard those rumors as well."

Where would a slave hear such things?

"Why do the Black Sentry trouble you?" Brita asked.

"Why else?" His voice dropped to a whisper. "I disobey the Laws and Ways of the Sentinel."

"Yes, but what in particular is your crime?"

He spoke while munching. "Possession of forbidden relics."

"You have Constructs?"

Drake grinned. "What's wrong with you, girl? You seem intrigued, almost pleased, at the prospect. Do you not fear Constructs? Do you not know they destroyed the world of Ancients?"

"I have heard that said," she replied.

"But you do not believe it?"

"I do not know—I—" She took a deep breath. "No. I do not believe it. And besides, it does not relate to my question. Do you have Constructs?"

"Have them? I make them."

She gasped. "And they work?"

"Well . . . that's more complicated . . ."

"How many do you have?"

"Several."

"Where are they?"

He swept his hand grandly in a wide arc. "All over."

"You don't keep them with you?"

"I couldn't keep them all with me. I couldn't carry them all, and if I tried, I would soon be apprehended. No, I have to be more cautious."

He was anxious to see more of these wondrous contraptions, like the Watch his father had shown him and the map and the books. He wondered if Drake truly had Constructs, or if the strain of exile had made him mad.

"If you have any Constructs with you," Brita said, "I should very much like to see them. Perhaps we could work together. Try to restore them, learn how they work."

Drake appeared interested. "Would you like that? Restoring relics?"

"I certainly would. I can read, you know."

"Indeed? How did you learn that trick?"

"I . . . came across some old books. Very old." He understood her hesitance to tell all. She did not want to incriminate her mother, especially to a stranger. "Do you have a Construct with you?"

"Of course."

"How near?"

Drake glanced up and pointed to a black bag behind the haystack.

"Will you show it to us?"

"Of course. Did you think I would take your food without offering you something in return? But it is very late. Perhaps tomorrow."

"No!" she insisted. "You did not wait to eat. Why should we wait to see?"

"Such enthusiasm." A tiny smile played on his lips. "Very well."

"What is it? Some sort of weapon? A transportation device?"

"I assure you, it is nothing so grand as that."

"Then what is it?"

"Flickers."


Daman and the others gathered in a small circle on the floor of the barn while Drake assembled his Construct. Various components were attached by a series of revolving twists that inserted one piece into another. Large wheels—Drake called them reels—were attached by spokes to the main contraption. Thin black glistening material spooled around the wheels.

"There," he said, after perhaps twenty minutes of assembly.

"That takes care of the projector. Now we need a source of light. Xander, do you have water in that canteen of yours?"

"Yes."

"Good. I have a vial of calcium carbide."

"Of what?"

"Just get the water."

Xander brought it to Drake, who poured it into a bucket and placed it behind the projector. Then they extinguished their candles. It was so dark they could barely see anything.

Drake took a vial from his bag and slowly poured it into the water. A small cloud of white smoke rose up . . .

And then, suddenly, a burst of blinding white light shone out of the bucket, brighter than the sun at midday.

"Don't look directly at the light," Drake said. "Look at the wall."

He thought Drake had lost his mind, but at any rate, he could no longer look at the bright light cast by the bucket.

"I'll have to crank this by hand," Drake said. "The Pulse prevents the motor from running."

"The Pulse?"

"Later, later." Drake turned a knob on the side of the projector. "Watch this, Daman."

He gasped, and he was not the only one to do so. He was glad to hear Brita and Xander were equally amazed. Otherwise, he might have thought he had lost his wits.

The projector cast pictures on the wall of the barn.

And the pictures moved.


Daman listened as Drake explained. The pictures on the wall told a story. He did not have the entire flicker, and he did not know the whole story, but he tried to fill in the gaps for them as best he could. Apparently there was a group of men who were good, and they were trying to infiltrate the headquarters of a group of men who were bad, so they stole the bad people's costumes and dressed up like them.

He had a hard time following the story, but Brita appeared entranced by it. What amazed him most was the view it provided of the world in which these people lived. It was like a window into the past, into a world that had died long before he was born.

The men in the pictures were nothing like anyone he had ever known. Their clothes were shiny, smooth and shimmering. Their tunics were bright gold and blue. The cities in which they lived had tall buildings that reached to the sky. They could travel from one place to another in the blink of an eye. They had a ship that carried them through the dark reaches of space. They had weapons they held in the palm of their hands that eliminated their enemies instantly. His blood raced, excited by this magical peephole into the past.

After a few minutes, the show ended. The light from the bucket faded, and the flicker came to an end.

"So that was the world of the Ancients," he said breathlessly. "What marvels they achieved."

"Haven't I told you as much?" Brita said. "Now you've seen it with your own eyes."

"What you saw," Drake interjected, "was not the world of the past. It was a portrayal of how the people of the past envisioned the future might be." He inhaled slowly. "They were wrong."

Brita suggested it would be best if they got some sleep. They were all tired.

He was exhausted, but he found that as he lay his head down on the hay, he did not sleep. His heart pounded and his head was filled with questions.

"Brita," he whispered.

"Yes?" she answered. It seemed he was not the only restless one.

"Are you awake?"

"Did you think I was talking in my sleep?"

"How did you persuade Xander to help you get me out of the Keep?"

"I didn't. It was his idea. He came to me for help."

"What?"

"He knew we were friends. He saw us in the alleyway, after the confrontation with Lieutenant Coffin. And apparently he saw you enter my house yesterday."

"But why would he—?"

"Xander was concerned about you. He was prepared to do whatever it took to set you free."

"I don't understand. Why would he do that?"

"Xander has always liked you. He's done everything imaginable to curry your favor. He dreams of being your friend."

His head was muddled. "I—didn't realize—"

"Perhaps you were too busy asking him to fetch your breakfast."

He fell silent. Her words stung, but he knew there was truth in them. All his life he had been taught to see slaves as just that. Slaves. Tools. Nothing more. He did not like to see them mistreated, but he never saw them as more than servants.

"Xander admires you," she continued. "Worships you, practically. Frankly, I don't see the big attraction, but Xander insists there's something special about you. That you have something others don't."

"Like . . . a Gift?" He remembered the Old Man's words in the cellar.

"I don't know what he sees. But I know he dreams that one day you will see him as a friend. Not as a slave."

"But Brita—we've always been taught that slaves are . . . well, not the same as us. Different."

"We're all different. Hadn't you noticed?"

"But that . . . deformity. On the side of their heads."

"What of it? You have a mole on the small of your back. It's not much to look at, but it hardly makes you less of a person."

His face reddened. How did she know he had a mole on the small of his back?

"Just try to be nicer to him, okay? He did save your life, after all."

"Brita," he said, after a moment, "I'm grateful for your help. Your and Xander's help. But you haven't been tried and sentenced. You haven't been declared an enemy of the Sentinel. They don't know who you are. You could still go back to the village. You could live a normal life." He hesitated. "You could marry Mykah."

She ignored the last comment. "They may not have known who we were before, but they surely do now. Someone probably recognized Xander or me or both during the chase. Even if they didn't, the Black Sentry spent the day going from house to house, waking people, searching their homes, trying to determine who's missing." There was a brief moment of silence. "No, we cannot go back."

"Brita . . ." he said, " . . . I'm sorry . . ."

"For what?"

"I've ruined your life."

"Don't be ridiculous. I was the one who decided to help Xander rescue you. I made the decision fully realizing what the likely consequences would be."

"You did that for me?"

She made a soft laughing noise that he did not much care for. "I did it for the Resistance."

"We should rescue the Old Man. Before the Ritual of Execution."

"I admit . . . I've had similar thoughts myself. But it can't be done. Especially not now, when the Black Sentry are looking for us. It would be suicide."

He tried to sound strong. "I would rather commit suicide than live knowing I left the Old Man in the clutches of the Black Sentry."

"It's impossible. When we broke you out, we had the element of surprise. But guards will be swarming all around the Old Man's cell."

"Then we won't go there."

"It *would* be wrong to just move on," she murmured at last, "without even trying to save him."

"Of course it would be."

"But we'll have to think this through carefully. We'll have to work out all the details in advance. We can't afford to make any mistakes. We will need a plan."

"Of course," he answered. "And if anyone can devise a plan that will succeed, Brita, you can."

"Do you really think so?"

"I know so."

She fell silent.

"So do you have any ideas yet?" he said, after a bit.

"I did have a thought," she said slowly. "About something I saw in Drake's flicker . . ."

# TWENTY-ONE

Daman and friends woke early the next morning. They found Drake was already gone, vanished without a trace. They gathered their belongings and resumed the journey to Clovis.

The rest of the trip was as exciting as the first part—perhaps even more so, because the sun shone and he could see everything, every bird, every bug, every blade of grass. He loved how each blade seemed individual and distinct, not flat and even and smooth like what they called grass back in the village. He kicked over a rock and found all manner of slimy creatures writhing underneath. He didn't know what most of them were, but he was entranced by the variety. The sameness of everything in the village was dull by comparison.

The only consideration that spoiled the excitement was the ever-present danger of Creepers. More than once they heard the chilling rattle that signified a monster's approach. By moving quickly, they managed to avoid them.

At one point, he attempted a conversation with Xander.

"Uh . . . Xander," he said, clearing his throat. "I . . . uh..wanted to . . . thank you."

"Thank me?" Xander said, his eyes widening slightly. "For what?"

"For yesterday. For saving me. Breaking me out of the Keep."

Xander shrugged. "It was nothing."

"I hardly think so."

"I was happy to do it."

"Yes. And I—I—" He swore silently. He knew what he should say, and this was the perfect time to do it. But every time he tried, he would glimpse that throbbing reddish bulge on the side of Xander's head and begin to feel ill.

"Anyway," he said, stiffening, "it was well done. You have my gratitude."

Xander nodded, and his face returned to the usual brooding expression.

By mid-afternoon they saw the tall walls of Clovis. From the outside, it looked no different than Merrindale, except larger. They found an unwatched spot and, using the rope and hook, managed to scale the fence and descend into the village.

By chatting casually with villagers, they soon learned that the Old Man had been tried and, as expected, convicted of treason against the Sentinel. The Ritual of Execution would follow tomorrow morning. What's more—the Acolyte himself was expected to preside over the ceremony.

While they talked to people in the village marketplace, he heard heavy footfalls coming from the vicinity of Clovis's Keep. Black Sentry.

They ducked for cover, without attracting too much attention. He thought the Clovis Sentry might have been told to watch for them. As he watched the platoon march in formation past them, he saw that the reality was much worse.

"Mykah," he said under his breath.

Brita nodded, but gestured for him to stay quiet. Mykah

marched near the front of the contingent. He must have traveled from Merrindale—with how many others? And why?

Near the end of the formation, he saw the purpose of the parade—transporting the Old Man. His hands were tied and a heavy wooden brace had been locked around his neck and shoulders. He looked exhausted. He had probably been forced to walk all the way from Merrindale, despite his injured ankle. He breathed heavily, and each step seemed to make him wince.

The crowd reacted as soon as they saw the Old Man. People shouted and cursed and called him ugly names. Some even threw vegetables. His heart sank as he watched the Old Man being so cruelly treated. He heard a Sentry explain that the Old Man was being transported from the courthouse to the Clovis Keep, where he would remain until it was time for the Ritual of Execution.

He exchanged a glance with Brita. Neither of them spoke, but he knew the same thought was on both their brains. They had to rescue the Old Man. Somehow. Before it was too late.

———

AFTER NIGHTFALL, from a safe hiding place, Daman saw Mykah emerge from the Clovis Keep. Keeping a discreet distance, he and his friend followed Mykah until they arrived at the temporary quarters provided for his stay in Clovis.

They waited until all the lights in the small cottage were out, and then waited even longer, until it was reasonable to assume that Mykah, and most of the people of this village, were asleep.

"Are you sure you can do this?" he asked.

Brita nodded, her eyes not quite meeting his. "I'm sure."

She hurried to the front door and knocked briskly. When there was no response, she pounded harder. A few moments later, they heard footsteps. Mykah was up, probably fumbling around for clothes.

A few moments later, Mykah opened the door. He wore a casual tunic and trousers—probably what he slept in.

"Hello," she said simply.

Mykah could not have looked more surprised if he had seen the Sentinel himself. "Brita. But—I was told . . ."

"Yes?"

"I was told you disappeared."

"I didn't go far. I spent the night in a barn in the forest."

"But—the Creepers! The Savages!"

"As you can see, I managed to survive."

"The Black Sentry said you joined the traitors. The Resistance. They said you helped Daman escape."

"Did you believe that?"

"No, of course not. But I couldn't deny that you disappeared. I thought that—that—"

"What?" Her voice took on a softer tone. "You thought what?"

"I thought you left to avoid me. To avoid marrying me."

Poor Mykah. Daman could not help but feel sorry for him. Even from where he crouched in the shadows, he could see the hurt and anguish in Mykah's eyes. He loved Brita.

"That is not why I disappeared," Brita said.

"But you said—and I could tell—"

"I'll admit I wasn't anxious to marry, but that had nothing to do with you."

"Then what?"

"I'm only sixteen, Mykah. It's absurd to think that I should settle down, should resign myself to nothing more than being someone's housekeeper and child-raiser. I mean no disrespect to you. But there's a world outside our tiny village. There's so much I want to see. So much I want to do."

A deep furrow crossed Mykah's forehead. "I don't understand. What exactly do you want to do?"

"I don't know. That's my whole point. I want to learn."

"The Sentinel has decreed that you shall be my wife."

"Yes," Brita said softly. "I know."

"The Sentinel knows what is best for us, Brita."

"The Sentinel knows what is best for the Sentinel. He cares nothing for individuals."

"Brita!"

"If he did, he wouldn't try to confine me to one village. Separated from people and ideas and boo—" Fortunately, she stopped herself in time. "The Sentinel does not want what is best for me."

All at once, Mykah took her hands in his. He pulled her close and gazed into her eyes.

"I do." He whispered the words, his eyes never leaving hers. "All I want is what's best for you. If you don't want to tend the house or raise the children, fine. All I want is you."

For some reason, Brita seemed to have difficulty formulating her response. "Mykah," she said finally, "will you walk with me?"

He nodded, and she led Mykah away from the cottage.

Daman and Xander didn't waste a moment. As soon as Mykah and Brita were out of sight, they crept out of the alleyway and hurried toward Mykah's cottage. They slid through the front door into the main room, thankful to be off the street and away from prying eyes. They did not light a candle or use any other source of illumination. At this hour, any light increased the risk of discovery.

They made their way back to the bedroom. A slim bed rested in the center with a medium-sized trunk at the foot. There was also a closet and a small wooden chest of drawers.

"Do you see it?" Xander whispered.

"No."

"We only have a few minutes."

He nodded. This was a fact of which he was well aware and needed very little reminding. "You search the trunk. I'll take the closet."

He opened the sliding closet panel and rummaged through the contents. He thought it would be quick and easy to sort through Mykah's belongings, given that he was only temporarily lodging here, but the darkness made any search difficult. One item of clothing looked much the same as another. Repeatedly, he had to remove items from the closet and hold them by the window to view them in the moonlight. This consumed too much of their extremely limited time.

After a few minutes, he finished examining the closet. Xander finished with the trunk.

"Did you find it?"

"No." Xander's frustration was evident, compounded by his anxiousness over the possibility that Mykah might return. They knew that Brita would stall, but no matter how much Mykah loved her, he would not want to be out this late with no legitimate purpose. A suspicious incident could prematurely end the career of anyone in the Black Sentry.

Together, they assaulted the chest of drawers. They tried not to disturb things, as they did not want Mykah to realize he had been searched, but it was difficult. They ransacked every drawer, but still did not find what they wanted.

"Perhaps it isn't here," Xander said, eyeing the front door anxiously.

"It's here. We just have to find it."

"It's brand new," Xander said. "Probably the only new clothing Mykah has had in years. Surely he'd hang it in his closet."

"Maybe he didn't want it to be in plain sight," he said,

thinking aloud. "If it's his most prized possession, perhaps he'd put it somewhere safer. Somewhere special. Somewhere out of sight."

He scanned the room. They had searched all the obvious places. He tried to think—where would he put his most prized possession? He remembered when he was a tiny boy, when he often brought home small treasures—colorful rocks or flowers, perhaps a found coin. And he always hid them in a box that he kept—

He crouched down on his knees. He lifted the edge of the bedclothes and peered underneath.

There it was.

He pulled out a small box containing Mykah's shiny new outfit. The uniform of the Black Sentry, complete with the eerie hood and goggles.

"Come on!" Without wasting a step, they started toward the front door. Barely a moment later, they heard shuffling noises out front.

They froze in their tracks.

Footsteps. And a voice.

Mykah was on the bedroom end of the house heading toward the front door—the only door—which was already within his sight. They could not exit by the bedroom window— the only window—without being seen.

They had no way to escape. And Mykah was on his way inside.

# TWENTY-TWO

Daman did not know what to do. There was no way they could possibly explain this. Mykah had said their former friendship would not stand in the way of his duty to the Sentry. No matter how much Brita protested, he would turn them all in. Or at least he and Xander.

He heard a shrill, high-pitched noise directly behind him. He was so startled he jumped into the air.

Xander was whistling, the prearranged signal to tell Brita they were still in here. Xander had the talent of whistling in such a way that it sounded entirely natural, like one of the bird-calls often heard in the village.

Listening at the door, he heard Brita's voice. She was trying to prevent Mykah from going inside the cottage.

He and Xander huddled by the window. It had a single glass pane that could be raised.

Slowly, carefully, Xander opened the window. It squeaked at one point and he stopped. Brita's voice rose in volume. She had heard the squeak and was doing her best to drown it out.

Xander opened the window the rest of the way, but at that instant, Mykah turned around.

They ducked out of sight just an instant before he would have seen them. What would they do now? From where Mykah stood, he could see both the front door and the only window. They had no way to get out.

"I can't let you leave me again, Brita," he heard Mykah say through the open window. "We're promised."

"I never promised anything," she replied. "Others promised for me, something they had no right to do."

"You speak so strangely, Brita. I don't understand what's happened to you." His voice became firmer. "But I will not let you go. If you attempt it, I'll sound the alarm and call in the Sentry."

A long pause ensued. "I promise you'll see me again. I can't promise I'll change my mind. But I can promise I'll see you again."

His voice softened. "How can I believe you?"

"You must believe me," she replied.

He heard a soft murmuring noise, but no more words. He couldn't resist looking. Carefully, he edged his head out the window . . .

She was kissing him.

In the embrace, she'd managed to turn Mykah away from the window. She saw his head poke out and, with the hand wrapped behind Mykah's back, waved for them to go.

He didn't need to be told twice. They scrambled quietly out the window. Despite their best efforts, they were not entirely silent. Mykah didn't seem to notice. Apparently he had other matters on his mind.

They climbed out of the house with their acquisition and moved stealthily toward their prearranged meeting point.

———

Daman waited impatiently for Brita to return. After about ten minutes, she appeared in the darkened alleyway. "Did you get it?"

He held up the uniform so she could see. "We did."

"Excellent. I couldn't keep Mykah away any longer. I tried everything imaginable, but he's very stubborn." She held the uniform up to the light. "With this, no one will question us inside the Arena."

"But how will we get there in the first place? During the Ritual of Execution, the Black Sentry will be everywhere. We can't simply walk through the streets. Someone will recognize us."

"I know how to get to the Arena without being seen," Xander said.

He looked at Xander incredulously. "How would you possibly—" He stopped himself. "But Sentry will be on every street corner, on every road—"

"They will not be in the tunnel."

"What tunnel?"

"There's a tunnel leading from the Arena to a place north of the village. Or may be. There was a tunnel in Merrindale. I've been told every village has one."

"I've never heard of this."

"It's a closely guarded secret."

"Then how would—"

"How would a mere slave know?" Xander's lips became thin and tight. "A slave would know because the slaves are the ones who do all the hard work that makes the Sentinel's 'miracles' occur."

He bit his tongue. "But how can it stay secret if slaves know?"

"What harm is there in telling a few slaves? After all, slaves are not even allowed to speak unless spoken to." He paused.

"What those fools don't realize is that if they tell one slave, they tell us all."

He didn't understand what that meant, but he had more pressing questions on his mind. "What's the purpose of these tunnels?"

"Have you never wondered how the Sentinel's men arrange those amazing disappearances when villagers are exiled or executed? Here one minute, gone the next?"

He remembered the latest example, when Mister Anton was sentenced at the Festival only a few days before. "We are told that the Sentinel's power—"

Xander rolled his eyes. "They drop through a hole in the floor of the Arena and are spirited away underground."

"A tunnel," Brita echoed. "Of course. It's obvious, once you know."

"There's a platform raised and lowered by a pulley. It makes people appear or disappear through the hole in the floor. After that, they're hustled out of the village through the tunnel. Never to be seen again." He paused. "But if we can find it, the tunnel could be used to spirit us *into* the Arena."

———

Taking care not to be seen, Daman and his friends returned to the village wall and climbed back out into the forest. They would have to wait until daylight to search for the tunnel. As always, they were wary of Creepers. They found climbable trees and nestled down, after agreeing they would take turns keeping watch.

He volunteered for the first watch. Brita and Xander settled in. He soon heard sounds that told him Xander was asleep. Apparently Xander could sleep anywhere, almost instantaneously.

Brita, however, was still awake. He gazed at her soft face, her yellow hair illuminated by moonlight. "Did you change your mind?" he asked.

"About what?"

"About joining the Resistance. Helping the Old Man."

"Of course not. Why would you think that?"

He looked away. "I thought perhaps you'd decided to stay with Mykah."

"Why? Because you saw me kissing him?"

"Well . . ."

"Daman, the only reason I kissed him was because you two fools got yourselves trapped in his cottage and couldn't get out."

"You shouldn't call Xander a fool."

"True. He hasn't been stupid enough to ask if I've changed my mind."

To his surprise, Xander laughed. "Leave me out of this." Apparently Xander was not as deep in sleep as he thought.

"You did not appear to be miserable while you were kissing him."

"Well, the ruse wouldn't have worked very well if I had, would it?"

"Most girls don't go around kissing boys they don't like."

"I kissed you, didn't I?"

That stung. He wished he'd had the sense to keep his mouth closed. "Kissing seems to be one of your favorite tricks."

"It's not my favorite anything," she shot back. "But I have noticed that once the lips lock, a boy's brain ceases functioning. That can be useful."

"Would you two stop already?" Xander said. "Sleep."

"Don't tell me what to do," he said, angry at the world.

"You've got no reason to be rude to me," Xander replied. "I didn't kiss her."

He could feel his face burning. "As if she would ever kiss—" He bit off the end of the sentence, but not, he realized, in time.

Xander rolled over, his face set in stone. "At first light, we must begin searching for the tunnel. Until then, I intend to sleep."

And eventually, they did.

# TWENTY-THREE

The tunnel was not as hard to find as Daman expected. So few people traveled between the villages, and so few knew about the existence of the tunnels, that great deception probably was not deemed necessary. A few fallen trees and leafy branches were strewn haphazardly across the entrance. Xander said it was much the same with the tunnel in Merrindale. Anyone looking for it would be able to find it. The problem was, few knew to look for it.

The tunnel was small, but large enough for them to pass through on hands and knees. It was cramped and dirty, and at times he had trouble breathing. He was surprised at how strongly it affected him. Sweat dripped from his brow and he felt a strange clutching sensation in his chest. He had never been in such a cramped place.

After they crawled a short distance, his throat went dry and he found he couldn't move. He felt as if the walls of the tunnel were closing in on him, as if he would be buried alive, deep under the earth. He knew these thoughts were not rational. But he could not banish them. He had to bite down on his lip to prevent himself from screaming.

"What's wrong?" Brita asked.

"N—Nothing."

"Why aren't you moving?"

His tongue felt so thick he could barely speak. "I—don't know."

He felt the touch of Brita's hand on his arm. It sent an electric charge through his already tremulous body. "I know," she said quietly. "I feel it, too."

"You do?"

"Yes. I don't know what's happening to us. But I know this —we have to keep moving."

He knew she was right. He was behind Xander but before Brita, and there was not nearly enough room in the tunnel for her to pass him. If he didn't move, Xander would be on his own. And he couldn't possibly succeed by himself.

The Old Man would be executed.

He took a deep breath, closed his eyes, and forced himself to crawl. He didn't need his eyes. There were no wrong turns he could take. He tried to imagine wide-open spaces, meadows, wheat fields, forests. Anything to take his mind off where he really was and what he was really doing.

As they traveled, Xander explained that although it was not known by most citizens, the Arena was actually a two-level structure. On top was the part everyone knew—the center stage where the ceremonies were held and the gallery where the villagers sat. But beneath that was a second level, an interconnected series of rooms and corridors used by the Black Sentry and a selected group of slaves. The tunnel would bring them to those rooms.

At long last, they detected a tiny dot of light in the distance.

"I think we're getting to the end," Xander said.

He had never heard sweeter words.

They crawled out, pushed through a hinged wooden door,

and closed the passageway. They were in one of the lower rooms of the Arena.

Quickly, they walked toward the center, Brita and Daman in front, Xander in back. It was not long before they encountered others.

The Sentry in the first room gaped in amazement. "The traitor!"

Two others jumped to their feet. "Seize him."

"That will not be necessary." Before anyone could do anything, Xander pushed Brita and Daman forward. "I have everything under control. Make way."

Xander wore the Black Sentry uniform they had liberated from Mykah the night before. Although he had never before worn anything other than a slave's simple costume, he seemed entirely natural in it. The hood covered the protrusion on his left temple. He'd tied Brita and Daman's arms loosely behind their backs and tethered to a rope Xander held firmly in his hand. To all appearances, they were two prisoners in Xander's custody.

The Sentry eased back into their chairs. "Where did you find them?" the first Sentry asked.

"In a barn outside the village." He pushed them harshly through the room, giving the impression that he had no time to stop and talk.

"But—how?"

Xander inflated his chest. "This is a matter of critical importance to the Sentinel's security. I will explain to the Acolyte himself and no one else."

"Of course. Proceed."

One of the men in the back leaned forward. "But the Acolyte is engaged at the moment. The Ritual of Execution is underway."

Xander snapped. "Do you think that I don't know that?"

"Of course, of course. Wait here while I make arrangements with the Captain of the Guard—"

"Are you mad?" He couldn't help but marvel at how well Xander handled himself. His imitation of an arrogant Sentry was perfect. He'd undoubtedly suffered many years of abuse at their hands. "Do you think the Acolyte wants me to *wait*?" His eyes locked onto the Sentry. "Do you think he'll be happy when he learns you've prevented me from informing him that I've captured the traitor and his accomplice?"

"Well—no—"

"If he learns now, before the ceremony is over, he can announce it to the people of Clovis. Imagine the joy and relief that will result. Would you spoil the Acolyte's opportunity to proclaim this glorious news?"

"Of course not." The Sentry nervously stepped aside. "Come this way. We'll lead you to the antechamber beneath the Arena. We'll be able to signal the Acolyte before he concludes the ceremony."

"Very well," Xander said. "Lead on. And be quick about it."

He concentrated all his powers on suppressing his smile and playing the part of the prisoner.

They were inside.

———

DAMAN and the others were led through a maze of rooms and corridors. He tried to take note of their route so he would be able to find his way out later, but he soon became hopelessly confused.

They passed more Sentry along the way, and each time the reaction was a condensed form of what they'd received from the first Sentry they met. First, seeing the supposed prisoners, they'd gape in amazement. Then, seeing Xander and being persuaded by his brash, confident manner, they'd step aside and let the party pass.

At last they arrived at the antechamber beneath the staging area of the Arena. It was a large round room filled with wooden rafters and support beams. He felt disoriented. He'd never seen a round room, a room without corners.

In the center he spotted a burly Sentry who stood before some sort of mechanism. He knew it was a pulley, but he had only the barest glimmer of how it worked. A wooden handle allowed a gear to be moved in a circular direction. A chain attached to the gear rose to the ceiling, passed through some interconnected wheels, then connected to a wooden plank fitting neatly into a hole in the ceiling of the room—which was the floor of the Arena.

Even though he did not perfectly understand how it worked, its purpose was obvious. As the man turned the handle on the gear, the platform would move. A man standing upon it would be raised or lowered. Add a cloud of smoke and this explained how traitors "disappeared."

The Old Man was not there. Apparently, he had already been raised to the surface of the Arena to await his sentence.

"Wait here," their Sentry-escort said. "The Acolyte will return soon."

"Very well," Xander snapped back. "I want all extraneous slaves and Sentry removed from the premises."

"But—"

"There are no buts," Xander said, cutting him off. "This is a matter of vital importance. I will not take any unnecessary risks."

Reluctantly, the Sentry gave the nod, and all but a skeleton crew of slaves left the antechamber.

He and Brita sat on a bench that allowed them to see and hear through a barred vent in the ceiling.

The Acolyte led the Celebration. Beside him, they saw the Old Man.

He was still alive.

They could also see that both he and the Acolyte were surrounded by a Black Sentry platoon. There was no chance they could snatch the Old Man without being seen.

The Acolyte conducted the Ceremony of Passage. All the villagers who had turned fifty during the past year were gathered together, honored, and granted passage. The Acolyte anointed them with the unction of transcendence, which symbolized their removal from village life and guaranteed them passage to Balaveria, the Sentinel's paradise. Their jobs would be assigned to younger men passing their Winnowing, while they were assured an eternity of pleasure and contentment.

Down below, Xander remained standing, pacing, making a great show of guarding his prisoners. But he noticed that the Sentry who had led them here did not depart. Perhaps he was not foolish enough to leave strangers so close to the Acolyte. Or perhaps he wanted to stay nearby so he could claim some credit in the capture of the prisoners. For whatever reason, he remained.

That was a problem, one they would have to deal with before they could try anything.

Through the vent in the ceiling, he saw that the Acolyte had finished the Ceremony of Passage but was not proceeding to the Ritual of Execution. Apparently he had some unscheduled business on his agenda.

"Children of the Sentinel," the Acolyte chanted, his arms outstretched, "we live in troubled times. I feel your unease. I know your unhappiness and fear. I know you worry about the enemies of the Sentinel, those who would destroy the Laws and Ways that we good citizens cherish."

"Long live the Sentinel," the people in the Arena shouted.

"Rest assured that the Sentinel cannot be defeated. He cannot be overcome. The Laws and Ways are the true ways. The only ways."

"Long live the Sentinel," the same voices chanted.

"And yet, the Sentinel knows you are troubled. He knows you sleep with fear in your hearts. And so he has sent you . . . this."

In the antechamber, two slaves loaded something onto the moving plank. It was at least twice the size of a man, but Daman could not make out what it was because it was cloaked. After it was in position, one of the slaves turned the gear handle and raised the draped object up to the Arena. From vents on all sides of the opening, an eerie orange smoke emerged.

"The Sentinel has been served for years by the Black Sentry," the Acolyte continued, "and they have served him well. But many of you have asked if there should not be more protection for the Sentinel in these troubled times. And so I introduce to you a new policing force, one certain to protect us all from the enemies of the Sentinel—such as he who stands before you now awaiting his punishment."

He grasped the bottom of the cloak. "Behold! The Silver Sentryman!"

The green cloak slid off, and along with the rest of the village he viewed for the first time what the Acolyte had unveiled. He did not know what it was—except that it was the most hideous, most frightening, evil-looking creature he had ever seen.

It was silver, from head to foot. Sunlight reflected off the shimmering surface, making it difficult at first to get a clear view. It was shaped like a man, a tall man, and yet it was clearly something else. It had a face, although that might be the wrong word. Its features were square and flat, unreal, suggesting human features but at the same time being nothing like them.

It reminded him more of a Construct than a man. The fact that it was so clearly not human but so unnaturally simulated human features, the cold eyes, and the huge size made it terrifying.

The Acolyte boomed forth in his most dramatic voice. "Come forth, Silver Sentryman!"

The hideous object on the platform moved.

The crowd gasped. There was a horrifying noise—part creaking, part whirring, part grinding. It set his teeth on edge and raised goose pimples on his skin.

One heavy foot lifted, then slammed down on the earth, making the ground shudder. The other foot did the same, then over and over again, gaining speed.

This unnatural creature could walk.

"Stop!" the Acolyte commanded, and the creature immediately obeyed.

The Acolyte turned proudly to face the crowd. "Children of the Sentinel, see what your kind and loving Master has sent to protect you. There is no escape from the Silver Sentrymen. They do not tire. They do not disobey. They cannot be fooled by trickery or lies. They are invulnerable to the weaknesses of the flesh. They can perform all the functions of the Black Sentry and more, but have none of their imperfections. They are unstoppable. Nothing can escape their control."

The crowd cried out—whether in relief or terror he couldn't be sure. As the noise of the people died, the voice of the Acolyte soared. "Let this be a lesson to all those who would transgress against the Sentinel. Let this be a warning to all those who would resist him or rebel against his Laws and Ways. Resistance is futile. Repent now, lest you face the unstoppable might of the Silver Sentrymen."

The Acolyte pointed toward a medium-sized wooden wagon on the floor of the Arena.

"Target the wagon."

Again they heard the horrible grinding and whirring noise as the unnatural man lifted its arm and extended it toward the wagon.

"Destroy it," the Acolyte said.

An instant later, a stream of blue-colored light burst out of the Silver Sentryman's hand. It flew across the Arena directly toward the empty wagon. The instant the light touched the wagon, it burst into flames. In a few moments it was completely incinerated.

Cries rang out from the gallery. Women screamed. People rose to their feet, clutching their children in their arms.

"The Sentinel has given this new Sentryman his own power to fight this holy fight," the Acolyte continued. "The enemies of the Sentinel will fall before his mighty hand. This is just one Sentryman, but more, hundreds more, will be created and scattered throughout the Sentinel's great empire."

The commotion in the gallery continued. More people rose, some in fear, some in panic. Some ran toward the back exit.

Watching from down below, Daman's throat went dry. These monsters must be the new enemy Drake had mentioned. How could the Resistance ever hope to defeat these invincible creatures?

"And now," the Acolyte said, "the time has come to deal with one particular enemy of the Sentinel."

He gestured, and the Black Sentry dragged forward the Old Man.

"It is time for your day of reckoning—Rico Dandel!"

The Old Man's surprise was evident.

"Yes," the Acolyte said, "I know your name. I know everything about you. You and all your traitorous companions in this so-called Resistance. You may wonder how I came by this information. Well, let me tell you then. Your friends gave it to me."

"It isn't true," the Old Man said, but his voice sounded weak and thin.

"Oh, they didn't give it to me right away, but eventually I was able to persuade them to talk. I know everything about you. Your Resistance is at an end." He turned back toward the gallery. "And should any other twisted traitors think to rise up against the Sentinel, they will meet their punishment too. At the hand of the Silver Sentryman."

The Old Man's eyes widened. He had undoubtedly expected death, but not to be obliterated by some unholy silver monster.

"Rico Dandel, you are cut off from the Sentinel and his people. Consider yourself shrouded." He snapped his fingers and several Sentry lifted the drape and placed it over the Old Man. It covered him completely, from head to foot. The wind blew the cloak back and forth, keeping it in constant motion around his body. He was maneuvered to the raised platform in the floor, presumably so his corpse could dramatically disappear after he was executed.

The Acolyte continued the ceremony, recounting a long list of crimes supposedly committed by the Old Man. The crimes were more numerous than anyone could possibly commit in a single lifetime. According to Brita, some of them occurred in places hundreds of miles away. It seemed the Old Man had become the scapegoat for any setback the Sentinel had suffered during the past several decades.

At last the time for the completion of the ceremony arrived. The Acolyte held his hands over the head of the draped Old Man.

"The Sentinel is a good and just Master," he chanted.

"The Sentinel is a good and just Master," came the response from the gallery.

"The Laws and Ways of the Sentinel are good and just."

"The Laws and Ways of the Sentinel are good and just."

"May the guidance of the Sentinel be with you, always."

"And also with you," the crowd responded.

"His will be done!" the Acolyte shouted. On that cue, the evil Silver Sentryman whirred into action. He pivoted, then walked a few heavy steps until he faced the draped figure of the Old Man.

More whirring, and the Silver Sentryman's arm rose till it pointed at the Old Man.

A collective gasp emerged from the gallery as the Acolyte shouted: "*Destroy the Rebel.*"

# TWENTY-FOUR

The instant the Acolyte spoke, Daman saw the deadly blue light burst out from the Silver Sentryman's hand. The instant the light touched the drape, it burst into flames.

Many of the villagers in the gallery turned their heads away. It was too terrible to watch. Even if the light did not obliterate the Old Man on contact, the heat of the flames would send him to a tortured, painful death.

Several moments passed in tears, horror, sadness. Until at last, one voice spoke. The voice of a child, a small boy seated on one of the lowest rows of the gallery. A boy brave enough to lift his eyes and his voice.

"Look!" the boy cried. "He isn't there!"

Every eye in the gallery turned. The Acolyte whirled around, as did the legions of Black Sentry surrounding him.

A fierce wind had blown the burning drape almost completely off the platform, exposing what lay beneath.

All they could see was a high-backed chair, one that had been tilted and wedged so that it straddled the hole in the floor and held the drape in place even after the platform was lowered.

The Old Man was gone.

———

A FEW MINUTES BEFORE:

Daman knew they needed to make their move quickly, but the Sentry and the slaves kept a careful eye on him.

"I need more rope," Xander said, addressing the Sentry who had remained. "Please fetch it for me immediately."

The Sentry's eyes narrowed slightly. "I think this would not be a prudent time to leave. The Acolyte might need assistance."

"The Acolyte will need rope. These are dangerous criminals. Go!"

The Sentry drew himself up. "No."

"I insist."

His lip curled. "I refuse."

"Very well then. I guess I'll just—"

Xander swung around, his fists clenched like clubs, and hammered the Sentry right in the face. The Sentry fell to his knees. Before he could respond, Xander hit him again, this time at the base of his skull. The Sentryman fell forward onto the floor and stayed there.

Daman's jaw dropped. He knew his slave was strong—but he had no idea how strong. All those years performing menial tasks seemed to have given him incredible physical power.

Brita tied and gagged the Sentry while Xander raced toward the two slaves who had remained in the room to operate the pulley.

"I am one of you," Xander said. He removed his hood so they could see the bulge over his temple. "And I need your help. Quickly."

They did not say anything, but their expressions changed. It was almost as if Xander continued talking to them, persuading them, even though not a word was spoken.

At last, one of them replied. "We'll do whatever you ask."

He couldn't believe Xander had been so successful so fast, but he didn't stop to question it. He knew they had precious little time. He climbed up the pulley mechanism till he was close to the ceiling of the antechamber. Xander passed him a tall high-backed chair.

He eased the chair beside the Old Man to hold the drape up as Xander lowered the platform. Fortunately, the constant movement of the drape in the wind disguised the substitution. Once the platform was low enough, he wedged the chair over the opening and helped the Old Man off.

"Daman!" the Old Man said. "Brita! And—"

"His name is Xander, and despite his uniform, he's with us. We must go."

The Old Man understood and followed them out of the room. He noted that the Old Man was able to quickly grasp the situation. He had far more experience running from the Sentinel than the rest of them.

They raced through the corridors as quickly as possible. Fortunately, they didn't encounter anyone. Presumably most people had gone above ground to see the Silver Sentryman in action. Unfortunately, the confusing array of passageways made it difficult to find their way back to the tunnel. They soon became confused. And lost.

"We don't have time for this," Xander said, teeth clenched. "The Acolyte will finish his litany and realize the Old Man has escaped."

They stood in the middle of a corridor with three choices— straight ahead, left and right. All the passages were dark and long. There was no way to see what lay ahead other than by trying them.

"I think it's this way," Brita said, pointing at the passage to the right.

"I thought it was the left," Daman offered. "Xander?"

"I haven't the slightest idea. But we must do something quickly."

He knew Xander was right, but he also knew a wrong choice would make it impossible to escape.

"Fine. We'll go my way," Brita said, tugging them to the right.

Something about the way she said it rubbed him the wrong way. "What makes you so sure you're right all the time?"

"We have to try something."

"Fine. Let's go my way."

"Don't be an imbecile."

"I'm tired of you telling me how stupid I am and how much smarter you are than everyone else."

"We don't have time for this," Xander reminded them.

"He's correct," Brita said. "We'll go right."

"Left."

"Actually, you're both wrong," a new voice said. "The exit is straight ahead."

They whirled around and saw not one but two Black Sentry behind them in the corridor.

"Thought you'd make another escape, is that it, traitor?" The Sentry stared at him with hatred in his eyes. He knew there was no hope of deceiving him. He had heard too much. "You were lucky once. You should have quit while you were ahead."

The two Sentry moved toward them.

Xander stepped in front of his companions. "You three go ahead," Xander said quietly. "I'll deal with them, Daman."

"No. We won't leave you."

"Don't be foolish. You must get the Old Man to safety."

He bit down on his lower lip. He hated the idea of abandoning Xander. But Xander was right—getting the Old Man back to the Resistance was their top priority now.

Before he could do anything, the two Sentry rushed them. Xander dove, letting loose a savage growl. He leapt into the air sideways and hit both of them broadside. They all clattered to the floor, Xander on top.

He did not doubt that Xander would defeat them. But it would take time.

"Come on," Brita urged.

Reluctantly, he followed.

They met no further interference as they wove their way through the corridors. The Old Man held up well, but his breath was fast and short, and his hand rarely moved from his chest. But he kept moving.

At last they arrived at the room connected to the tunnel.

"Great," he said breathlessly. "Now all we have to do—"

He stopped. A lock hung on the tunnel hatch. The tunnel was closed to them. And that was the least of their problems.

A young man blocked their way. He held a huge club, and his expression made it clear he did not intend to let anyone pass. They knew him to be a member of the Black Sentry, even though he was out of uniform.

He was out of uniform for a reason.

It was Mykah.

# TWENTY-FIVE

Daman stared at his old friend and saw nothing but hatred in his eyes.

Xander ran up behind them. It seemed he had dispatched the two Sentry. When he saw Mykah, he slammed to a stop.

"That's a fine uniform you're wearing, Xander," Mykah said, his lip curled.

Xander made no reply. He suspected Xander was sizing Mykah up, determining whether he could take him, despite the enormous club.

"You have all transgressed against the Laws and Ways. You have betrayed the Sentinel." Mykah peered at Brita through narrow eyes. "And you have betrayed me."

Brita stepped forward. "It was necessary, Mykah."

"Necessary? Necessary to become a criminal? A traitor? To make a joke out of everything? Including us."

"Mykah . . ."

"How do you think this makes me look, Brita? I want a career in the Black Sentry, the defenders of the Sentinel. And my own betrothed openly defies the Laws and Ways."

"I meant no offense against you."

"Last night." Mykah took a deep breath. "Last night you led me to believe there was some hope. That you cared for me . . . at least to some small degree."

Brita made no reply.

"But now I see that was all a ruse. A trick you played. So you could steal something that didn't belong to you and give it to a slave."

Brita walked toward Mykah, stopping when she was but a few feet away from him. Her voice dropped so low he could barely hear what she said. "Mykah . . . it was not . . . all . . . a ruse."

His head twitched. "It wasn't?"

"You're a fine boy. Any girl would be happy . . ." She paused. "It has nothing to do with you. It's me. I can't settle down to a life of dusting the farmhouse and watching the children. I just —I can't explain it properly." She shook her head. "I've always felt that there was more that I could do. More that I was supposed to do. Until this week, I didn't know what it was. But now I do."

"You plan to join this Resistance?"

She nodded her head.

"I took an oath," Mykah said. "An oath of allegiance to the Sentinel. I swore that I would enforce his Laws and protect him against his enemies. You've befriended the Sentinel's greatest enemy."

At that instant, they heard a commotion from the Arena—shouting, crying, running. He knew what it meant. The crowd —and the Acolyte—knew the Old Man had not been incinerated.

If they were going to escape, they had to go now.

"They'll be here soon," Brita said, peering into Mykah's eyes. "If they capture us—you know what will happen."

She moved even closer to him. His hand brushed through her stunning blonde hair.

"Just answer one question," Mykah said. "Last night, when you told me—what you told me. Was that the truth? Or was it another lie? Another trick you played so you could get what you wanted?"

He could not help but wonder what she had said, but no explanation was forthcoming.

"That was the truth, Mykah. I meant it. I still do."

His face softened. "I'm glad. What I said last night was true also. All I want is what's best for you." He lowered his club, still gazing into her eyes. "Go."

"Mykah—"

"Go. Before I change my mind." He turned toward Xander. "Do me the favor of clubbing me over the head on your way out."

A strange request, but they all understood why he made it.

"Wait!" Brita ran forward suddenly, threw her arms around Mykah's neck, and kissed him on the cheek. "Thank you," she whispered.

A brief smile flickered on Mykah's lips. "Quickly, Xander."

Mykah closed his eyes and Xander knocked him in the head with the club. Mykah fell to the floor. He probably was not unconscious—Xander had not appeared to put any great effort into his blow—but it would leave a mark sufficient for him to claim he was overcome.

Xander beat at the lock on the tunnel door but he could not get it open.

The Old Man gazed at the tiny tunnel door. "I doubt," the Old Man said softly, "that I could make it through that tunnel in any case."

Daman knew what that meant. They would have to take to the streets.

They raced outside. They were relieved to see that the Black Sentry had not yet surfaced. They ran toward the north wall of the fence at top speed, helping the Old Man along.

As they pulled away from the Arena, he saw several Black Sentry platoons cascading out the main entrance. Curiously, however, the Sentry did not race after them. They seemed to collect in the marketplace, falling into a loose formation. He could not imagine their reason for not pursuing, but he was not about to stop and ask, either.

They reached the wall and used the rope with the metal hook to scale it. They all managed to get over the fence in record time—even the Old Man. After that, they darted toward the north road.

By the time they reached the road, they had not met a single Black Sentry. They walked for a good while without interference. He thought they were either enormously clever or uncommonly lucky—when he heard the voice.

The voice boomed through the air, rustling branches and frightening birds out of trees. "*Stop, enemies of the Sentinel!*"

The Old Man gripped his arm tightly.

"What was that?" Xander murmured.

Again the booming voice split the air. "Your efforts are futile. There is no escape."

None of them had ever heard such a thing. The voice seemed unconnected to any person, any body. It seemed to descend from the sky.

Brita looked at him. He knew what was in her mind.

It was as if the Sentinel himself spoke to them.

He turned to the Old Man. "Have you ever heard anything like that before?"

"I have not. But I have spoken to others who have. The Acolyte has a Construct that amplifies the voice. Makes it louder."

"But Constructs don't work—"

"You're wrong. Constructs do work. But only if the Sentinel wants them to work."

"Then the Sentinel—"

"The Sentinel is nowhere near here. The Acolyte has the device. He's trying to scare us."

If so, he thought, the man is doing a fine job of it. "What can we do?"

"Ignore it. He's nowhere near us and neither are his minions. We must hurry."

They continued running. They followed the north road and soon crossed another bridge over a wide river. As soon as they had crossed, however, the voice returned.

"Your efforts are futile," it bellowed. "You have no hope of escape."

"Don't let him disturb you," the Old Man said. "He cannot see us. He is not here. There's nothing he can do."

"Prepare to suffer the fate that awaits all enemies of the Sentinel," the voice continued, even louder than before.

"I think we should run," he said.

"Yes," Xander replied. "But where? From what?"

"Defenders of the Sentinel," the voice boomed, "*engage!*"

At that moment, they saw why the Acolyte was so confident they would not escape, even though the Black Sentry had made no effort to pursue them. Ahead on the road, just peeking over the horizon, they spotted a splash of silver glistening in the sunlight.

"Oh, no," he whispered.

"We've lost," Xander gasped.

"Not them," Brita said. "Anything but them."

On the road before them, they saw the monstrous Silver Sentrymen.

Three Silver Sentrymen. Heading straight for them.

CHAPTER

# TWENTY-SIX

In the fading light Daman saw and heard the heavy footsteps of the inhuman Sentrymen. They walked at a slow but steady pace. Their eyeless heads focused straight ahead, never moving.

He knew what the beams of light coming from those monsters' arms could do. He did not wish to see it demonstrated again. Especially not on his friends.

"Turn around!" he shouted. "We'll go back the other way."

Brita looked at him as if he had lost his mind. "Back to Clovis?"

"Better that than the Forest of the Savages."

She didn't argue. All their lives they had been taught about the Savages and their filthy, barbaric lifestyle . . . and their taste for human flesh.

They headed back toward the village. Unfortunately, they had barely gone two hundred feet when, once again, they saw menacing glints of silver just above the horizon.

Three more Silver Sentrymen. Coming at them from the other direction.

The Silver Sentrymen blocked the road on both ends.

There was nowhere they could go.

The nearest Sentryman raised its arm. As if targeting them.

"We must leave the road," the Old Man said.

"What about the Savages?" Brita had the same expression on her face as when she first spotted a Creeper.

"We have no choice. Come on."

The Silver Sentrymen continued their steady march, lurching forward with earth-shattering footfalls.

The Sentryman closest to them pivoted, following their movement.

Before, in the Arena, he had noticed a bright red light in the Sentryman's hand that glowed just before the deadly blue beam of light emerged. Now he saw the red light again. As soon as it began to shimmer, he dove and rolled close to the ground.

The Sentryman's deadly blue beam of light blasted out where he had stood only seconds before. It struck a tree, which instantly burst into flames. He covered his ears, blocking out the sound of the explosion. Smoke billowed up. Large chunks of leaf and bark flew all around him.

He could feel the heat, even as far away as he was. "Quickly," he said. "Into the forest."

This time, his companions did not hesitate. The Silver Sentrymen fired all at once. Hot beams of blue light crisscrossed all around them. They struck the ground and the trees, sometimes ricocheting in different directions. One beam hit another tree, sending large wood chunks flying through the air. Another beam blasted just over their heads.

He ran, making sure the Old Man and the others kept pace, never looking back.

Until he heard a sharp cry of pain just behind him.

He whirled.

The Old Man had been hit.

He and Brita ran to the Old Man's side.

"It wasn't the blue light," the Old Man muttered. Sweat poured from his forehead. "Some of the flying debris—" He gritted his teeth. A hole seared his tunic. Although there was no bleeding, his chest was severely burned.

He and Xander lifted the Old Man to his feet. The Sentrymen's beams were still firing. They couldn't afford to stop until they were much further away.

Fortunately, although the Silver Sentrymen were lethal and terrifying, they did not move that quickly, especially off the road and in the forest, where the ground was not flat and the way was often blocked by trees.

The Old Man's eyes were wide and his gasps were short and strained. His hand clutched at his chest. He appeared to be having trouble breathing.

The Silver Sentrymen attempted to pursue, but because of their enormous size, they were unable to pass through the densest parts of the forest. A few more beams of blue light flew over their heads until finally they were out of range.

The more they ran, the more the heavy footsteps of the Sentrymen fell behind them, until finally they could not hear the monsters at all.

———

DAMAN CARRIED the Old Man deep into the forest, not resting until the sun set. Once he felt sure they were safe, he gently laid the Old Man down in a bed of leaves. They removed his tunic. Xander poured water from his canteen over the wound. Other than that, there was not much they could do. After a few moments of stillness, the Old Man's eyes closed and he seemed to rest.

"Do you think he'll make it?" Brita asked.

"I have no idea. We need to get him to a physic. But we can't go back to Clovis."

"And the nearest village beyond Clovis is at least two days' journey." She held the map in her hand. She had been studying their options.

"I've scouted the surrounding area," Xander said, "and I saw no trace of the Sentrymen."

"The Silver Sentrymen may be powerful," Brita said, "but they are not fast. And they were not made for trudging through forests."

Xander nodded. "Although it may be simply that . . . they felt they had no need to follow us into the forest."

They all knew what he meant. There was no need for the Sentrymen to follow their prey into the forest—because with Savages lurking everywhere, they were already as good as dead.

They heard a weak, tremulous voice behind them. "Are we safe?"

Brita ran to the Old Man's side. "We're safe. At least, from the Sentrymen."

He nodded. Some color returned to his face. He was undoubtedly still in pain. He winced when he spoke. But the brief rest seemed to have done him some good.

"Do you mind . . . if we talk about the Sentrymen?" Brita asked.

The Old Man did not show great enthusiasm for the subject. "If you wish."

She hesitated. "They weren't . . . *real*, were they?"

"They seemed very real to me."

"Yes, but—they weren't . . . natural, right? They were Constructs."

The Old Man nodded.

Xander drew in his breath. "If that's what Constructs were like, I can see why the Sentinel eliminated them."

"No, no," the Old Man said. "Remember what I said before. Constructs are neither good nor evil. They're tools. Even before the Sentinel, they merely did what those controlling them wished."

"The controllers?" Xander asked. "The privileged class?"

The Old Man shook his head. "In the time of the Ancients, everyone had Constructs. *Machines.* Some more than others, yes, but everyone had them. There were machines that could perform every imaginable task or chore. There were machines that cooked your food, cleaned your house, transported you from one place to another. The Ancients were always thinking up new machines, machines that could do even more than those that preceded them."

"Was this bad?"

"Not really. But it worried some. Not everyone believed in progress. Some clung to the past, insisting life was better long ago. There are always such people, in any era, who think the time of their youth was the best and the world has deteriorated ever since. But toward the end, just before the Sentinel's rise, there were more than ever before, because life was changing so quickly. New inventions seemed to arrive on a daily basis, and strange new experiments were constantly increasing knowledge, leading to even more new discoveries. Information was exchanged at lightning speed. With new knowledge came new power. And power in the wrong hands is always dangerous. Some scientists uncovered the fundamental secrets of life itself. People experimented, and of course, some of those experiments went wrong. It was rumored that the Creepers were the result of experiments gone bad."

"You mean," he asked, "the Creepers did not exist in the time of the Ancients?"

"No, not until the very end of the time before the Sentinel. At first, there were only a few Creepers, but they proved so unstoppable and reproduced so quickly that they soon spread to every unprotected corner of the continent."

"And the Savages? Did they exist in the time of the Ancients?"

"No," the Old Man said, but there was an odd expression in his eyes. "The Savages definitely did not plague the Ancients."

"Were there other experiments?" Brita asked.

"Indeed. Of many different varieties. But the most frightening, perhaps, were those performed on people themselves. Some scientists thought to make humanity better than it was, to improve it. Some of those results were astounding—but the results of others were terrifying. And they remain with us today."

"But—" Xander said, "even the slaves had machines?"

"There were no slaves," the Old Man said. "Not at the time of the Sentinel's ascension. The great evil we call slavery had existed for millennia, but the Ancients finally eradicated it. Men and women were free. Until the rule of the Sentinel began."

"What kind of freedom?" Xander asked.

"Women could choose their futures for themselves," Brita said.

"Everyone could choose their futures for themselves," the Old Man said. "They could make virtually every decision themselves. Chart their own future. They could decide where to go and when to go there. They chose their own occupations, their own spouses. They could live anywhere they wanted and move any time they wished."

Daman listened with amazement. He still could not conceive of a world with so much freedom of choice. "It must have been wonderful."

"In many respects, it was. But sadly enough, it made many powerful people uncomfortable. There were some who disliked having so much freedom, or more accurately, disliked it when others had so much freedom. When humans are free to choose for themselves, inevitably, some choose poorly. That can cause hardship for others, especially those who think the whole world should be a reflection of themselves. They called for stricter rules, a return to the past, more centralized control. Increased ability to monitor the activities of those who were different. And it was only a short step from monitoring activities to dictating activities. 'Order' became the watchword of the day."

"'Order' is the watchword of the Sentinel," he noted.

"It certainly is. Order from chaos." The Old Man took a deep breath. "There was great debate. Opposing forces did a lot of shouting. This went on for years, no one getting anywhere. For every person who wanted stronger controls, there was another who wanted to retain freedom. It was a stalemate. Until the Sentinel came along."

"And then?"

"The Sentinel took up the banner of those who fought for Order. And unlike the others, he had a means of bringing his vision of the world into reality."

"By killing the Constructs?" Brita asked.

"Yes. Don't ask me to explain it. I'm no scientist. It was like he cast a spell over the entire realm—and the Machines stopped working. The Ancients, so unused to doing things for themselves, rapidly fell apart. In the madness and chaos that followed, it was easy for him to seize control. He took over, establishing his Black Sentry as a ruthless police force and himself as indisputable ruler."

"And suppressing freedom," Xander said quietly.

"Of course, the Sentinel claims he has not suppressed freedom. He claims that when all people have unlimited freedom no one is free—each is limited by the impositions of others. He claims that by structuring society along stricter lines and guiding citizens in the important decisions that affect the welfare of the entire community, he gives each person the freedom to make their highest and best contributions to society."

"Do you believe that?"

"No. It's a lie. A lie told by every despot since the dawn of time. There is no freedom in this world the Sentinel has made. People's ambitions, their hopes and dreams, their aspirations, all are crushed in his all-controlling grip. That is why we must fight him, even though the odds seem impossible. We must fight him and fight him and never stop fighting him."

"How can the Sentinel still be alive after so much time?"

"That's a mystery that has baffled us."

"And the Silver Sentrymen—?"

"Are machines. And somehow they work, even though no one else's machines will." His eyes closed. Brita told the two boys to move away and let him get some rest. He would need it, she said, if he was going to endure the next day's journey.

Xander opened his pack and shared what little food was left. Some water, some bread, a smidgen of cheese. Obviously, they could not go far unless they found more.

"Perhaps we can find food in the next village," Xander suggested.

"Even if we could, how would we buy it?" Brita asked.

"There are other ways to get food than buying it."

They gathered some leaves together and tried to make reasonably comfortable pallets on the ground. They had not seen or heard any Creepers, and the Old Man clearly could not climb, so they decided not to go into the trees. One of them would stay on watch throughout the night while the others slept.

The Forest of the Savages was frightening enough during the day. But in the black of night, it sent shivers up his spine.

Steeling himself, he agreed to take the first night's watch, while the others nestled down to sleep. He paced around the perimeter of the clearing, keeping his eyes and ears open. Eventually, Brita and Xander drifted off. He paced around their encampment, trying to stay alert . . .

When he first heard the sound.

He whipped his head around, trying to see what caused the rustling. Was it Creepers? Or worse? He listened and watched, trying to detect any trace of their distinctive slithering movement.

He saw nothing. But he knew he'd heard something. And even if he couldn't see it . . . somehow, he sensed it. There was something out there.

Slowly, he made his way to Xander's pallet. "Get up," he said, under his breath. He gave Xander a gentle kick.

Xander blinked his eyes a few times, then came around. "What is it?"

"I don't know. That's the problem."

Xander woke Brita, and the three of them gathered in the center of the clearing.

"Are you sure you didn't imagine it?" Brita asked. "Forests are full of living creatures. It could have been a bird, or a squirrel, or—"

She stopped in mid-sentence. They all heard the noise this time, coming from somewhere beyond the clearing.

"What if it's a Creeper?" Xander asked.

He knew what Xander was thinking. What could they do to escape a Creeper? They couldn't possibly get the Old Man up a tree in his current condition. And how far could they carry him?

The faint sound seemed to grow closer.

"I don't think it's a Creeper," Xander said.

"Well, that's a relief," he replied. Except it wasn't. Because if it wasn't a Creeper . . . the next most likely alternative was even more frightening.

All at once, the trees surrounding them came alive. Dark shadow figures leapt out of the brush, shouting and crying. They were tall, dirty creatures, wearing little or nothing and chanting at the top of their lungs, words he didn't begin to understand. They circled around him and the others, trapping them. The circle slowly contracted. The hideous, rhythmic chanting grew louder as the threatening figures drew in upon them.

He had no doubt about who or what these terrifying creatures might be.

Savages.

CHAPTER

# TWENTY-SEVEN

Daman whirled around in circles, trying to find a way to escape from the Savages. But there was no way out.

The Savages carried long staffs, many of them sharpened like spears. He also noticed that many of them wore ornaments around their necks—necklaces strung with teeth and bones. Beyond that, they were all but naked and black as the night.

"It's true what they say about Savages, isn't it?" Xander shouted over the din.

"Will they kill us?" Brita asked.

Xander's face was grim. "And then devour us."

The frenzied shrieking of the Savages intensified. They bounced and whirled and danced, keeping time to some primitive rhythm only they could hear. It was a terrifying spectacle.

The Savages were so close now he could smell their revolting breath. They twisted and writhed around him, contorting themselves grotesquely. Some of the Savages poked him with their sticks. He slapped them away, but he knew it was a futile effort. There were far too many of them.

"I am sorry," he said, looking into Brita's eyes. "I wish I had never—"

He was interrupted by a new voice behind him. "What's going on?"

It was the Old Man. All the noise must have wakened him.

The circle of Savages widened a bit as some of them turned to take in the Old Man.

"Run!" Daman shouted. "Before they surround you!"

But the Old Man did not run. He did not appear terrified, either. To the contrary—he smiled.

"Honestly, Will," the Old Man said. "Couldn't you do that a little more quietly? I was trying to get some sleep."

All at once, the Savages stopped writhing and chanting. They pulled back, dropping their sticks on the ground. The horrible chanting and writhing suddenly gave way to—laughter.

And the Old Man laughed, too.

"I don't understand . . ." Daman said.

"I think I do." Brita took a step forward. "You're not really Savages, are you?"

One of the Savages smiled—bright white teeth in a darkened face. "You're wrong. We are the Savages."

The next one over jabbed him in the ribs. "We're just not very savage Savages." Again, they all exploded with laughter.

"It's a ruse," Brita said. "You're covered with mud. And all that chanting and writhing and poking is just to frighten people."

The first Savage looked at the Old Man. "She's a smart one, Rico. Where'd you find her?"

"It's a long story."

"And you aren't cannibals, are you?" Brita continued. "And you aren't primitive."

"True," the Old Man said. "But the jewelry was a nice touch. Are those real teeth?"

The first Savage shook his head. "Paste."

"But all the stories," Xander said. "All the grim tales of the horrible Savages. I've heard them all my life."

"Then we've done our job well."

"But if they're not Savages—who are they?"

The Old Man laid a hand on his shoulder. "They're the people you're so eager to join. The Resistance."

Brita's eyes lit. "Then—they're soldiers?"

The Old Man shook his head. "Scientists."

———

AFTER THE LEADER of the pack of "Savages"—whose name was Will—and the Old Man talked for a few minutes, they led Daman and his friends back to their headquarters. It was not far away—a short distance compared to the journey they had made already. He was amazed to find that the so-called "Savages" were regular people, just like anyone else—except that they were covered with mud and nearly naked. He listened intently as they talked. Half of the words they used he did not understand.

Eventually, they arrived at the entrance to a cave in the side of a mountain. The entrance was disguised by brush and fallen trees, but the Savages—or rather, the Resistance—soon cleared the way.

He gaped as he stepped inside. The interior was huge. He could see why they had chosen it for their base of operations. Although the space was vast, it was virtually invisible from the outside. He supposed it had to be, to elude the prying eyes of the Black Sentry.

As he walked through the cave, he saw many other men and

women. For the most part, people remained silent and focused, watching the Old Man and waiting for him to speak.

"Bad news," he heard the Old Man say to one of the other Resistance leaders. "Those rumors were true. The Silver Sentrymen are a reality."

"But how do they avoid the Pulse?" Will asked.

"I don't know."

"Then it's hopeless."

"No. But it's more important than ever that we strike immediately."

"But how?"

Without a word, the Old Man reached into Xander's pack and withdrew the beautiful red stone. The Key.

"You succeeded." He clapped the Old Man by the shoulders. "You got it."

"Yes." He looked at his friend levelly. "So you see, we have a chance. A slim one. But a chance, just the same."

He noticed that the mood inside the cave changed dramatically when he revealed the key. He felt a sense of guarded optimism—of hope.

After the Old Man conferred with the leaders, Will gave them a tour of the headquarters. With his Savage disguise removed, he had a kindly face and a thick brown beard. Will appeared to be perhaps a few years older than his father.

"So," he said, "I suppose it will soon be time for you to make the journey to Balaveria."

"I certainly hope not," Will replied.

What did that mean?

Will showed them the entire Resistance complex. Daman learned that, in addition to the vast central room of the cavern, there were various smaller caverns used for other purposes. They saw the Rebels' sleeping and living quarters. They saw the planning room. They saw the stockpile room—which was filled with Artifacts from the past.

He raced through that room like a treasure trove, gazing slack-jawed at the wide variety of devices. "And all of these things date from the time of the Ancients?"

"All of them," Will confirmed.

There were machines of all sorts and sizes—some so big they looked deadly, some so small he couldn't imagine that they could possibly do anything.

"May I touch them?" he asked.

Will nodded.

Daman picked up a small thin glassy sliver. "What is this?"

"That was a phone," Will explained. "People used it to talk to one another."

"Does it work?"

"Not now. The Pulse prevents it. But at one time, it allowed people to communicate over great distances."

This revelation interested Xander. "People could talk—even if they were far away from one another?"

"Exactly. And not just talk. It could transmit music, signals, even pictures or information."

Xander nodded quietly.

They continued wading through the piles of artifacts, holding items up for Will to identify, wondrous objects called tablets and freezers and computers. Sometimes, even Will didn't know what a particular machine was. Sometimes, he knew what it was supposed to accomplish, but had no idea how it was done.

"Much knowledge was lost during the Great Darkness that came during and after the Sentinel's battle for control. We're trying to recapture some of that lost knowledge, but it's slow work."

Finally, Will insisted that they move to a room he called a

laboratory, filled with vials and small fires and other unfamiliar objects. Will explained that the scientists worked here, trying to recapture the greatness of the Ancients—or invent some of their own.

"There's one other room I want you to see," Will said, leading them onward. "One I think may be of particular interest to Brita."

Brita walked eagerly behind him. "And what is that?"

Will outstretched his arm and pushed open a door. "The Library."

Brita's jaw dropped.

Back home, she had seven books. Here in the Library—they had hundreds.

Brita raced up and down the shelves, gazing at the spines and covers. "I can't believe it," she said breathlessly. "I never dreamt that so many books even existed." She gazed at the covers. "Books on agriculture and animals. The stars and fighting techniques and—" She grabbed one and clutched it to her chest. "Science!"

Will smiled. "And a million other subjects you've never even heard of."

Her eyes watered. "All these books," she said, "all this knowledge. It's just—it's too good to be true." She looked up at Will tentatively. "Perhaps when I'm older, under close supervision, I might be permitted—"

Will laughed. "You can check out a book whenever you like. That's the whole point of a library."

For once, Brita was speechless.

"All you have to do is sign the card in the back, so we know where the book is in case one of the scientists needs it. Then you can keep it as long as you like."

Tears actually spilled down her face. Daman was amazed. She had faced the Black Sentry, the Acolyte, the Creepers, even the Silver Sentrymen, without losing control. But now she cried. Over books.

"Thank you," she said quietly. "Thank you so much."

"Wait a minute," Xander said, as he peered out the library door. "I think I see someone we know."

All three whirled around in the direction Xander was pointing.

"Drake!"

They ran toward him. Drake smiled as they approached. He held out his arms and gathered them up in a great group hug.

He seemed entirely different from the man they'd met in the barn. There was no more of the ducking and hiding, the skittering twitchiness. Here in the scientists' sanctuary, he was perfectly at ease.

"I'm so glad to see you all here," Drake said.

"Then you're one of the scientists?" she asked.

"Didn't I tell you that when we met? That I invented things?"

"Well . . . yes, but—"

Drake laughed. "But you didn't really believe it, because I acted like a crazy man? Don't feel bad. That's what you were supposed to think. I tried to do the Savage routine, but I was never very convincing. So I went with the lunatic act."

"Why were you out on your own?" Daman asked. "Isn't that dangerous?"

"Extremely. But someone has to do it."

"Why?"

"Reconnaissance, my boy. Reconnaissance of the past."

"I'm afraid I don't understand."

"Have you seen the library yet?"

"We certainly have," Brita said. "It's extraordinary."

"You're right. But it didn't collect itself. It only exists because I—and others like me—have roamed the countryside, searching, collecting. And not just books. All those artifacts you saw in the storage room. Machines. Relics. Hard drives."

"Are you making . . . a museum?" Brita said, mispronouncing a word she had only read in books.

"Oh, much more than that, my dear. We collect relics because we hope to use them."

"Is that possible?"

"Our goal is to gather up the knowledge of the Ancients so we can restore or recreate their technological marvels. With the strength of these tools, we hope finally, someday, to break free of the Sentinel's iron grip."

He felt his heart beating faster. So that was the plan. That's what all these scientists and laboratories worked toward.

"Come with me, my friends." Drake took them back to the laboratory, showing them projects and experiments, introducing them to friends, explaining everything patiently. He was surprised at how many people were there. Most had escaped from their birth village, but some had slipped through the Sentinel's grasp for generations.

Drake took them to a part of the lab he called the foundry and tried to explain how they made metal. Basically, they took ores mined from the ground, heated them, mixed them, then let them harden into molds that gave them new shape. There were other steps involved, but Daman couldn't grasp it all at once. His lack of comprehension made him feel insecure. The only thing that made him seem more insecure was watching Brita nod and smile with understanding.

He noticed that the metal was being molded into small rectangular metal boxes. Although the work was slow, they had already made dozens of them. "What's the purpose of the black boxes?"

Drake answered. "That's our newest project. We're making a weapon."

Brita seemed to understand what he meant. "You mean like—a gun? Like we saw in your flicker?"

"Similar. Guns are far more complicated—they require powder and bullets and complex firing mechanisms. And they're potentially lethal. The weapons we're making would stun attackers, but not kill them. Rather than propelling a lead bullet at high speed, it would transmit an electric charge. The opponent would be incapacitated for a while but would suffer no lasting harmful effects."

"How do you generate the electricity?" Brita asked.

Drake seemed impressed that she knew enough to ask the question. "Batteries. We've been working on them for years now, but as you can see we only have a few finished stunners. We have few hands and mining is hard work. And it's difficult to construct an electrical machine when you can't test it."

"Why can't you test them?" Brita's brow wrinkled.

"They should work. I'm confident we followed the blueprints correctly. But the Pulse prevents them from functioning."

"The Pulse? Is that how the Sentinel prevents machines from working?"

"Exactly. And it's a shame, because we need those weapons. We're planning a major assault on one of the Sentinel's fortresses, and we can't put it off any longer, weapons or no weapons."

"Why must you act now?"

"I think you already know the answer. You've encountered them yourself."

"The Silver Sentrymen."

"Correct. If those automatons spread throughout the land, we'll never be able to overthrow the Sentinel."

"Do you know where they're being made?" Xander asked.

"We certainly do. Balaveria."

His lips parted. "Balaveria! But—Balaveria is paradise."

"Balaveria is a prison camp," Drake said grimly. "When the men and women of the villages reach the age of fifty, the Sentinel eliminates them from the village work force, so they can be replaced by younger and more productive workers. Those from this region are shipped to Balaveria, where they're forced to perform repetitive menial labor to keep the Sentinel's evil operations running—maintaining his machines, building new ones, powering the Pulse. And they continue doing that demeaning work until the day they die."

"But—all my life—"

"Lies," Drake said, not even waiting to hear the end of the sentence. "Like so many others the Sentinel has propagated."

He was overwhelmed just thinking about it. He had seen so many people go through the Ceremony of Passage. Now he was told they were not headed for paradise but to a slave ring. And yet, he did not doubt what he heard for an instant. He felt the same certainty he'd had regarding other disclosures made to him the past few days. Horrible as it seemed, something inside him told him it was true.

"Why are the Silver Sentrymen made at Balaveria?" Brita asked.

"Because that's where the workforce is," Drake replied.

"But why is the workforce there?"

"Because Balaveria is the source of the Pulse for this region."

"I have heard so much about this Pulse," Brita said. "But I don't understand what it is."

"The Pulse is a phenomenon discovered long ago by the Ancients," he explained. "The records we've uncovered suggest that the discovery was almost accidental. It was a side effect of a great weapon the Ancients created, one that split the fundamental building blocks of matter itself to unleash vast destructive energy."

"Why would the Ancients want such a horrible device?"

"The Ancients' world was far from perfect. People wanted weapons, sometimes to fight, sometimes in the hope that having such weapons would prevent future fighting. At any rate, this particular weapon was discovered to have a strange side effect. It emitted what was called an electromagnetic pulse."

"And what did that do?" Daman asked.

"It made everything stop working. Every kind of machinery. Anything that had any magnetic or electrical mechanism. Any kind of engine. If it was within the range of the Pulse, it ceased to function. The Sentinel discovered a way to make a Pulse without the bomb. He broadcast the Pulse like a blanket so it covered the countryside. He developed a machine that would constantly emit the Pulse so that it never faded."

"And that's why the Constructs stopped working."

"Except the ones he wanted working. He created a shield that immunized his own machines from the effect. Suddenly, no one's machines worked—except the Sentinel's. You can imagine what happened after that."

"The Sentinel took control," he said. "Easily."

"No one could oppose him effectively, when he was the only one with functioning machines. Once he had the land firmly within his control, he eliminated all machines from public view. He wanted to turn the clock back and create an artificial world of the past, a time when life was supposedly simpler and better. None of it was real. It was an egomaniacal tyrant's fantasy of the way the world once was, the way the world should always be. With mass-produced reproductions of nature."

"Once we left the village walls," he said, "the world seemed very different."

"Of course it did. Outside the villages, the world has not been reshaped into the Sentinel's nostalgic vision. But inside the village, it's an orderly fantasy. An amusement park for the

Sentinel's amusement. The villages differ from one region to the next, but they are all equally artificial. So much time has passed since the Sentinel took control that most people don't realize life was ever different. They think the Sentinel's way is the only way. They can't imagine a life of true freedom. That's what we must change."

"If you could stop the Pulse, you could use your stunning guns," Brita said.

"That's true—but it's much easier said than done. The Pulse is emitted from four fortresses positioned throughout the Sentinel's land. The one that covers our region is located in a tower at Balaveria, only about two hours walk from here. The tower is surrounded by a high stone wall—a fortress."

"Is it possible to turn off the Pulse?"

"It is now. Thanks to you three."

The Old Man entered. He looked much better than he had when they saw him last.

"Because you and your friends had the courage to rescue this." In the Old Man's hand he held the glittering red stone he had once worn around his neck. "This is the key to restoring the freedoms and marvels of the Ancients. The means of ending the Sentinel's cruel reign and establishing a better world for humanity."

"How does it work?" Brita asked.

"Mind you," the Old Man said, "what I'm telling you now has taken us decades to learn, years spent reading and rereading the books of the Ancients, the science books and the history books, even sending spies into Balaveria. We learned that the tall central tower of Balaveria has hidden, in its highest and most inaccessible room, the machine that broadcasts the Pulse. We also learned that there's a device that would turn the Pulse off—this key. The Sentinel reasoned that the day might come when he chose to turn the

Pulse off, but he didn't want that power to fall into the wrong hands. For that reason, the Acolyte kept the key with him at all times."

"Until you stole it," Xander said, grinning.

"I didn't work alone," the Old Man replied. "I worked with four others, friends of mine." His voice dropped. "Friends who did not return from the mission. And the Sentry would have caught me too—if it hadn't been for you, Daman."

He felt light-headed. He thought he'd done the right thing by helping the Old Man. But he'd never exactly realized why, or how important it was—until now.

"Balaveria is always well-guarded," Drake explained. "More Black Sentry platoons than you've ever seen swarm the fortress. Over a hundred men. There are only about fifty of us, even assuming we all joined in an assault. And the Pulse generator is far from the entrance—deep inside and high up in a tower with few windows and only a single door."

"But we can't wait any longer," the Old Man said. "Even if the odds are stacked against us, we must act now—or everything we've worked for so long will be lost."

"There must be some way to get in," Daman said.

"Don't think we haven't thought about it," Drake replied. "We've worked this problem from every angle imaginable. But we've never come up with a solution."

He pondered a moment. "What about some kind of airboat?"

Drake arched an eyebrow.

"In Brita's books," he continued, "she showed me pictures of great carts that transported people over long distances through the air."

"An airplane would be perfect," Drake agreed. "It could fly over the walls of the fortress directly to the tower. If we could sail over the heads of the Sentry guarding the front gate, we might stand a chance. But we don't have the means to build an airplane. And even if we did—"

"The Pulse," Brita said somberly. "The Pulse would prevent the engines from working."

"It's true. We experimented with the possibility of building a glider, an airplane without an engine, one that floated on air currents. But we didn't have adequate materials or knowledge. And we couldn't figure out how to get it into the air. There are no cliffs or plateaus near Balaveria to launch from. And there were a million other problems. The truth is—it was beyond our capabilities."

"There must be some way," he insisted. "When we were in the forest, I saw birds. They flew. And they do not have engines."

The Old Man smiled. "That's true. But unfortunately, we are not birds. And I don't think the sparrows are likely to give us a lift."

"There must be some answer." Even though he had no idea what that answer might be, he wasn't willing to give up. "You need some kind of flight that isn't a machine. That doesn't have an engine."

Brita turned to face him. Her eyes were wide as saucers. "Daman—that's it!"

"What's it?"

"What you said. You're right—we need an air machine that doesn't use an engine. One that can launch itself."

"Is there such a thing?"

"There is," Brita said. "And as it happens, I'm an expert on them. I've been experimenting for weeks. I showed you, back in Merrindale." Her eyes were wild and excited. She grabbed the Old Man by his arms. "You don't need an airplane. You need a balloon."

# TWENTY-EIGHT

Daman was amazed at how quickly they made progress from that moment forward. Plans were drawn for the assault on Balaveria, and he and his friends were at the center of them. They'd brought with them not only the Key, not only information—but also hope. For the first time, all the Rebel leaders could visualize the possibility of success. A slim possibility, perhaps, but a possibility, just the same.

Drake and his team of scientists were at first dubious about Brita's idea of constructing what he called a "hot air balloon." On this subject, she was actually more knowledgeable than the scientists.

"You do know what a balloon is, don't you?" she asked, that first day the idea arose.

Drake did not answer immediately. "But how could that help us? A balloon is a child's toy—"

"Not that kind of balloon," Brita said hastily. "One large enough to carry people aloft."

"Is such a thing possible?"

"It is," Brita said emphatically. "The Ancients did it. And I've done it—on a smaller scale. With your help and your resources, I'm sure we can make it happen."

Their first steps were into the library. They divided into teams and systematically combed every book on the shelf, searching for information about hot air balloons. He tried to help as best he could, but since he could not read, his contributions were obviously limited, which he hated. More than ever before, he was determined to understand those scratches. He wanted to learn what they had to teach him.

By the end of the first day, they'd researched every book available to them. Early on, they found several pictures of hot air balloons, huge constructions with baskets capable of carrying half a dozen people, which eliminated the question of whether such a thing was possible. The only question now was whether they could make one. They found a few short articles pertaining to hot air balloons, but nothing very detailed, nothing with as much information as the book Brita had been forced to leave behind in Merrindale. But she had read it—more than once.

From that point forward, Brita was the leader of Operation Airlift.

He watched attentively as they conducted several experiments to determine whether they could make something similar to what the scientists called "nylon." As best he understood, this was an artificial fabric that was tough but light, easy for the hot air to lift aloft. Unfortunately, it was beyond their technological capabilities. They would be forced to use cloth, light and thin as possible while still strong enough to be dependable.

While Brita led the construction of the balloon, Xander spent his time with what came to be called the "ground assault team." Not every Rebel was a scientist, as he soon learned (to his great relief). Some Resistance members hadn't learned to read or had no real talent for science—including Will, who became the ground assault team leader.

The assault team spent the first several days reviewing charts of the fortress of Balaveria. Xander soon knew it as well as if he'd lived there all his life. Will pointed out a high outcropping of rock that would cover them until such time as they were ready to attack. Once they broke from cover, Will advised that they should make a frontal assault on the north fortress wall. True, the front wall was likely to be the most heavily guarded, but the only opening in the wall, a ten-foot-tall gate, was in the center. If they could get some of their team over the wall or through the door, the rest could storm the fortress. They might even be able to use their stunners—

Assuming the balloon got off the ground. Finding enough cloth to make a sufficiently big balloon was not easy. Many people gave up all their spare clothing, even the shirts they were wearing. Stitching it all together was also a problem. Brita had emphasized that the balloon had to be what she called "airtight," meaning there could not be even the tiniest of openings through which air might escape.

Eventually enough cloth was gathered and the stitching began in earnest. He was pleased to find that sewing was a talent he could master. It might not be science, but he was glad to make a contribution.

The first tests were not successful. They built huge bonfires, trying to generate hot air to fill the balloon. But they found that the air was difficult to direct and control. Every time they filled the balloon, they realized it was not airtight, which meant stopping and sewing on another patch.

He began to wonder if this contraption would ever hold air. He noticed that Brita was also pensive. Although she did her best to hide her concerns, much rested on her thin shoulders.

While Brita oversaw the construction of the balloon, Drake

worked on the stunners. He believed it was urgent that they attack Balaveria before another week passed. Their spies indicated that another fleet of Silver Sentrymen—a larger, faster, deadlier version—would be produced soon. They had to strike quickly. To that end, he stepped up production of the stunners as much as possible. It was his goal to have one weapon for each member of the ground assault team. He knew they would face strong opposition. He wanted to do whatever he could to even the odds.

As the stunners rolled out, Xander and the other members of the assault team practiced using them. An obstacle course was laid out, and the team members practiced running, ducking, and firing all at once. They did everything imaginable to become proficient in their use—everything except actually firing them, since that was impossible. For all the hopes they pinned on these little black boxes, they knew one thing with absolute certainty—if the balloon team couldn't shut off the Pulse, the stunners would be useless. And they would never know if they really worked—until everyone's lives depended upon them.


DAMAN'S CONFIDENCE in the Rebels turned out to be well founded. Eight days after Operation Airlift commenced, they had a functioning balloon. It was a crazy, patchwork bulb made of a hodgepodge of colors and fabrics, but it had held air for more than a day. It was smaller than they had planned. The basket attached was only large enough for two passengers. But it seemed to work. They held a series of tests, cautiously raising the balloon and lowering it, using bags filled with dirt for ballast. They even practiced steering—a little. The balloon remained tethered to the ground by a rope. Any more extensive testing was not practical. Even in this remote part of the forest, if the balloon took to the air, there was a strong chance some Sentry somewhere would spot it. That would not only tip off the Sentinel's forces that an attack was coming, but would probably cause the area surrounding Balaveria to be flooded with Sentrymen. They couldn't take the risk.

Under Brita's tutelage, he learned the basics of operating the balloon. A fire would be built on a brazier in the center of the basket. The heat from the fire would inflate the balloon and eventually lift it into the air. Bags of dirt would be tied to the sides of the basket. They could be released at any time if they needed to rise quickly. Using a perforated metal board, they could cover the fire in whole or in part when they wished to raise or lower the balloon.

At the end of the eighth day, after the balloon had been sent through a rigorous series of tests—and passed them all—a council convened in one of the small chambers of the cavern. All the Resistance leaders were present. Drake, representing the scientists, attended with a few of his chief assistants. So did Will, on behalf of the ground team, with Xander at his side. The Old Man was also present. Brita was of course present, being the driving force behind Operation Airlift. He had also been invited, although he had no idea why. For most of the past week, he'd felt utterly useless. Brita was smart and knowledge-able. Xander was strong and fearless. But what could he possibly contribute to the assault?

Will laid a map of Balaveria in the center of the table and carefully walked everyone through the plan, step-by-step. When he was done, there was a moment of somber silence.

"How certain can we be of this plan?" the Old Man asked.

"As certain as possible," Will answered, "given the countless uncertainties involved."

The Old Man leaned back in his chair, his hands steepled. "This could be a turning point in history. For the first time since the Sentinel rose to power, the oppressed will make a concerted effort to break free of the shackles he has used to chain us. If this effort fails—who can say what the future holds? There may not be another such opening for hundreds of years. Perhaps never."

"But we have to take the chance," Drake urged.

"We're gambling with more than our own lives," the Old Man continued. "We're gambling with everyone's lives. Everyone's future. If we try and fail, there will be severe repercussions."

"If we don't try, there will be repercussions," Drake insisted. "The Silver Sentrymen will blanket the countryside. After that happens, there will be no possibility of freedom for anyone."

The Old Man nodded. "I know. I just wish we could act with more certainty. You say this balloon is capable of carrying a Rebel to the high tower?"

"Yes," Brita answered. "All our latest tests have been successful."

"But you have not actually taken the contraption into the air without a tether."

"No."

"You don't really know how it will perform up in the sky. This creates yet another uncertainty. As will our reliance on the equally unproven stun guns."

"I've constructed those weapons with the utmost care," Drake said. "I've followed the blueprints to precise detail."

"But you haven't tested them."

"You know that's not possible."

"Which creates more uncertainty."

The table remained silent for a long moment.

Drake finally spoke. "I suppose, Rico, that in this instance . . . we must simply have faith."

The Old Man touched his collar. "We must have faith," he agreed. "Since it's all we have. Let's hope it's enough."

"I have a question," Will said. "Who will pilot the balloon?"

"I will," Brita replied, not giving anyone a chance to answer differently. "I have the most experience with balloons."

"That makes sense," Will agreed. "But the basket beneath the balloon has room for two people. For your own safety, I think you should take a co-pilot."

"Agreed," Brita said. "I will take Daman Adkins."

Daman's jaw dropped. She hadn't said anything to him about this . . . but it helped explain why she'd spent so much time showing him how the balloon worked.

Will seemed puzzled and, perhaps, concerned. "I bear no ill will against your friend, but—why him?"

"Because I trust him."

"Surely you would be safer with a seasoned member of the Resistance. Someone with more experience who—"

"Who has more experience than Daman at defying the Sentry? And escaping them?"

Daman's face colored. He was unused to hearing others talk about him in such a complimentary manner. He felt embarrassed—but pleased. Especially since the words came from Brita.

"Daman and I have already been through so much together. We work together well. He's sometimes rash and imprudent, but I'll be along to keep that in check. He's brave and he can keep his head together under pressure. I've taught him the fundamentals of controlling the balloon. I know he'll do well. I choose him for my co-pilot."

Will didn't say another word aloud, but motioned the Old Man to one side. They spoke quietly, but he was still able to hear most of what they said.

"Rico," Will whispered, "is this wise?"

"It's her choice to make," the Old Man replied.

"But she's so important to our mission. I worry about her safety."

"Daman is a very responsible boy."

"But they're both so young."

"It's right that he should be with her. He has the Gift."

That ended the conversation. They returned to the table. "Are we all in agreement, then?" the Old Man asked. His eyes scanned the conference table. One by one, each representative gave him a nod.

"And are we all ready to proceed?"

Again everyone nodded in agreement.

"I don't need to remind you that we face incredible odds," the Old Man said. "We're attempting to do something that has never been done before. But I have faith in you—all of you. And I have faith in what we seek to achieve. Goodness and right are on our side. Even if we fail, we will not have acted in vain."

He laid his hands flat and pushed himself up from the table. "My friends—it is time."

# PART THREE

THE ASSAULT

# TWENTY-NINE

Daman had no trouble waking early the next day because he barely slept.

The next morning, before daybreak, the Resistance team began its assault on the fortress at Balaveria. During the night, a small cadre lit bonfires and began the process of inflating the balloon. By morning it was ready to travel, and the wind blew in the right direction. Drake and his team of scientists checked the ballast and made last-minute adjustments. Will and his ground assault team waited for instructions to march. They would leave first so they could be in position before the balloon arrived.

Standing on a small rise in the center of the clearing, Daman saw the Old Man quietly overseeing everything. There was a light in his eyes and excitement in his voice—but also, he noted, a certain sadness in his expression.

Before he left to join the troops, Xander approached he and Brita. "Best wishes," he said. He took Brita's hand and clasped it tightly.

"And the same to you," she replied. "Success."

Xander nodded, then sidestepped to face his former master.

He cleared his throat awkwardly. "I—uh—hope all goes well for you."

"Of course. We will all do our best."

He noticed Brita's eyes burning down on him. He knew what she wanted. Xander was reaching out to him, aching to be his friend. And once again, he pulled away. Perhaps if he . . .

Too late. Xander rejoined the rest of his team. A moment later, Will and his troops disappeared into the forest.

"You know," Brita said, "you may never see him again."

"I know."

In the past few days, his world had been turned upside down. So much that he had been taught about the Sentinel, about the Rebels, about Balaveria, had turned out to be false. And yet, with each new revelation, he'd managed to adjust. In fact, each time he learned something new, from the Old Man, from Drake, from the Resistance, he seemed to instinctively understand that it was true.

With one exception. He couldn't stop thinking of Xander as a slave.

"Do you think you'll have a problem with great heights?" Brita asked.

His brow wrinkled. "I would prefer not to fall from great heights, if that's what you mean."

"Please try to be serious. This is important. Some people fear heights. I've read about it. It causes nausea, dizziness. Do you think you might be one of them?"

"Why would you—"

"I remember when we were in the tunnel. You didn't take well to small, enclosed places." He couldn't deny that. But surely this would be different. At least, he hoped it would be.

"Oh well," Brita said. "We'll know soon enough. By the way —happy birthday."

Her words took him by surprise. It seemed like an eternity

since he left Merrindale. But in fact, as he traced their progress backward in his mind, he realized—

She was right. Today was his sixteenth birthday.

"Interesting way to celebrate, wouldn't you agree?" Brita said, tilting her head toward the balloon. "Still, it's got to be better than the Winnowing."

He had almost forgotten about the dreaded event that had been his principal obsession for months. He spent so much time practicing with Mykah—and losing. Now his friendship with Mykah had been severed. Mykah was the enemy, another cog in the black machine that opposed everything the Resistance hoped to accomplish.

He had avoided losing the Winnowing—by running away from it.

"It's time," Brita said, pointing toward the balloon. "Climb aboard."

———

WITH SOME EFFORT, Daman hoisted himself into the small wicker basket. As soon as they were both on board, the tethering ropes were released, and the balloon glided up into the sky. Brita controlled the fire, carefully covering it and uncovering it to lift and guide the balloon. Despite her lack of experience flying without a tether, she steered with precision and accuracy. The wind was strong and in their favor, promising to bring them to Balaveria even sooner than they expected. He hoped the ground troops were ready.

Brita kept the balloon as low as possible to prevent it being spotted from a distance. Every so often a tall tree or outcropping of rock would come into their path. She would do everything she could to maneuver the balloon around it. More than once, he thought they were not going to make it, only to have her lift the balloon at the last possible moment.

He quickly understood what Brita meant when she talked about fear of heights. Everything seemed different up here. Different and disorienting. The trees below were like twigs. The people were tiny colored dots, ants scrambling around anthills. It was like a tiny model of a world. And it was so far down . . .

He turned away and crouched down in the basket. His stomach churned.

For some perverse reason, Brita smiled. "My books were right," she said, apparently pleased. "You look a bit green."

"Green?" he croaked. His throat felt dry.

"In the face. Don't worry. It will pass. If you think you're going to be sick, though, please hang your head over the edge of the basket."

He peeked over the side and almost instantly felt his stomach churning again. Would the whole journey be like this? He didn't feel able to fight a mouse, much less the Black Sentry. He imagined himself falling, falling, and finally splattering on the ground . . .

He looked away. Right now he would give a great deal to be on solid earth. Even if he had to be inside a tunnel.

He noticed Brita struggling with the fire.

"Is there a problem?" he asked.

"No. I'm fine."

"You don't look fine."

"It's—just—harder than it looks. Easier when you're tethered to the ground. That's the problem with not being able to practice in the air."

He offered to help, but she said there was nothing he could do, and he supposed that was probably correct. His part would come later, when they reached the tower. He touched the glittering red key that hung around his neck.

They enjoyed several moments of calm, pleasant sailing. Then he saw a black shimmering cloud hovering before them. "Up!" he cried.

"What?" Brita said. "What is it?"

"Up! Or down. Quickly!" Too late. An instant later, they were surrounded by birds. A huge dense flock of them. He didn't know what kind they were, but they were large and solid black, and there appeared to be hundreds of them.

They were everywhere, all around them, smashing him in the face, crashing into the balloon.

Crouching for cover, he had a horrible thought. "Brita—what if they damage the balloon?"

Brita didn't answer. He presumed she thought he already knew the answer to that question. Which he did.

The birds whipped around the basket in a bizarre frenzy. The balloon spun, swinging wildly back and forth.

He clutched his gut. He'd felt queasy before, but this was something else entirely. He didn't know how much of this he could stand.

And then he felt the bottom drop.

"What's going on?"

"I don't know." Brita said. "But we're falling."

And falling fast. An upward current of air whipped his face. He'd left his stomach somewhere far behind, but he knew he had to ignore that and try to help Brita. Because at this rate, they would soon hit the ground, just as he'd imagined. Falling, falling, falling . . . and then splattering down hard.

"Did they puncture the balloon?" he shouted. The whipping wind made it hard to talk.

"No," she shouted back. "But the fire is down. Some of the birds crashed into the brazier."

He scooped dead birds out of the brazier, then poured on more firewood.

Brita glanced over the edge of the basket. This time, it was her face that looked green. "If we don't get that fire up quickly, we're dead."

"I'm working on it."

Together, they poured all the coals and wood they had into the brazier. The small flame licked against the fresh fuel. The fire increased, but slowly.

"Use the flint!" Brita cried.

Daman fumbled with the flint but it was hard work. Brita should've chosen Xander, he thought. Xander was much better at this than he was.

He managed to toss out a few sparks. The fire grew. He felt the descent slow till the balloon fully inflated again. With a huge whooshing sound, they shot back into the air.

And not a moment too soon. Glancing over the edge of the basket, he saw that they were barely above the treetops. A few more moments and they would've been dead.

"Thank goodness that's over," he said, wiping his brow. "How much longer do you think until we—"

His question was answered before he asked it. Across the horizon, plainly in view, he saw huge, tall, serrated walls, black walls that extended as far as the eye could see. It was a fortress the size of a village, strong and impregnable, with a gleaming black tower dead in the center, a tower that rose so high it looked as if it touched the sky.

It could only be one thing. Balaveria.

They had arrived.

Xander spotted them first.

"Look!" he said, pointing up at the sky. "They've made it."

Will and the rest of the ground assault team turned their heads upward. They crouched out of sight, hidden by a rock outcropping about two hundred yards from the front gate of the fortress. The last safe haven. If they moved any closer, they would be spotted by the patrolling Sentry stationed inside the high fortress walls.

The journey had not been a long or difficult one. They had not encountered any Creepers or Sentry squadrons. But Xander knew he was not alone in his uneasiness about the impending battle. Their success was critical to so many. But their plan had too many gaps, too many uncertainties. Too many things that could go wrong. There would be danger at every point—and no one would be more vulnerable than the hapless ground team, trying to combat an enemy secured behind tall stone walls. If this did not proceed according to plan, they'd be destroyed.

A slave was not normally called upon to take initiative, to make decisions for himself, to plunge into danger. But today that would change. He was determined not to shrink from the challenge.

The balloon arrived, an unmistakable patchwork bulb sailing across the sky. They were early. The balloon was much too low, barely higher than the fortress walls. The Black Sentry stationed inside could not help but see it. And when the balloon was this low, it was vulnerable to attack.

"Up," Xander whispered under his breath. "Get it higher."

Will placed his hand on Xander's shoulder. "We're all thinking the same thing," he said quietly. "But I don't think she can hear us."

Nonetheless, Xander kept his gaze fixed on the spinning balloon rapidly approaching the fortress walls. "Up," he repeated. "Rise."

———

"We've got to get this balloon higher," Daman said urgently.

"Do you think I don't know that?" Brita shot back.

"Is there anything I can do?"

"Not unless you can reduce your weight instantaneously." She dropped ballast bags, lightening the load. "Those birds did some serious damage."

"Perhaps we should turn around. Come back later. If they see us now—"

Too late. He heard a loud cry beneath him. He leaned over the edge of the basket and saw three Black Sentry posted along the wall of the fortress. One pointed into the air—directly at the balloon.

"We've been spotted."

"We're in the air. What can they do to us?"

He didn't know, but he feared they might be more resourceful than he was. "We have to rise higher."

"I'm doing everything possible. I'll get us to the tower windows. It just takes time."

Which was the one thing they didn't have. More of the Sentry gathered. The front gate opened. A horde of Black Sentry poured out.

"They're leaving the fortress," he said.

"Why would they leave the safety of the fortress?"

They had their answer soon enough: for ammunition. The Black Sentry combed the area outside the fortress, picking up rocks and sticks, anything in sight—and throwing them at the balloon.

A large jagged rock whizzed by his head. "We must get higher."

"We *are* higher!"

"Not high enough." A large stick sailed past him, lengthwise like a spear. It was sharp on one end. It could easily have punctured the balloon. "Can't we go any faster?"

"We're rising as fast as we can, but—*ahhk*!" A rock thudded into the small of Brita's back.

"Are you all right?"

"Fine," she said, gritting her teeth and tossing off another ballast bag.

The balloon rose faster now. Soon they were high enough that, even if a Sentry was strong enough to pitch a rock that high, it was unlikely to do any damage.

"Thank goodness," Brita said, massaging the sore spot on her back. "Soon we'll reach the tower windows. Until then, we should be safe."

"I'm not so sure." He leaned over the edge of the basket.

"What do you see?"

He tried to think how to describe it. Another Sentry squad had emerged, and the leader held something in his hands, something with a semi-circular shape and a thin shaft through the center. He didn't know what it was. But the hollow feeling in the pit of his stomach told him it was probably a weapon.

"Let me look." Brita moved to the edge of the basket.

"I'm worried about the Sentry standing on the—"

"I see him." Her voice was oddly flat.

"Do you know what he's holding?"

"I certainly do. I've seen many pictures in my books. It's a bow and arrow."

The words meant nothing to him, but he felt a clutching at his heart just the same. "Could this . . . bow and arrow harm the balloon?"

"Oh yes," she said quietly. "Oh yes."

———

Down on the ground, Xander saw the archers line up on the fortress wall.

"But how could it harm them?" Xander asked.

"I'm no scientist," Will replied, "but I know the bow acts as a means of propulsion. It can fling the arrow up. And the arrow has a sharp point."

"It could puncture the balloon?"

"Or worse—it could puncture Daman or Brita."

Xander's jaw clenched. "We must attack now."

"We can't. Our stunners are useless. We have no weapons."

"Daman and Brita have no weapons. We can't just sit here while the Black Sentry kills them."

"We must wait until the Pulse is disabled. That's the plan."

Xander saw the leader of the Sentry draw back his bow. The arrow shot up into the air. Not only did it reach the balloon—it actually flew too high, missing the balloon by inches.

"If we don't act fast, they will have no opportunity to disable the Pulse." Xander pointed toward the front of the fortress. "The gate is still open. Some of the Black Sentry are dawdling outside, watching the show. We'll never have a better opportunity."

He felt a strong hand clamp down on his shoulder. He turned to see who was behind him.

The Old Man had come with the ground assault team to observe—although all parties agreed he was too valuable to put at risk in the actual battle.

"We must stick to our plan, Xander."

"But Daman and Brita are in danger."

"I know how you feel, son. I never like seeing my friends at risk either. Nonetheless, we must keep to our plan. Everything depends on it."

"But—"

The Old Man held up a finger. "I'm sorry, Xander. We will wait."

———

"Get us out of here!" Daman cried. He'd seen the first arrow pass overhead, too close to the balloon.

All the ballast bags were gone. They'd sailed over the fortress walls, but they were still several feet from the tower windows. "I'm trying," Brita said, "but the wind isn't cooperating."

"Never mind the tower. Just get us away." He watched as the Sentry leader put another arrow in his bow and fired it. The arrow soared forward, coming so close he ducked. The arrow lodged in the basket. "Hurry!"

"Now we've gone too high," Brita muttered. "We're above the tower."

"There is no such thing as too high right now." He watched the Sentry load another arrow. "We must—"

Before he could finish, the arrow soared upward, making a high-pitched singing sound that stung his ears.

And the next sound he heard was a hiss.

He stared up at the balloon. "Does that mean what I think it means?"

She nodded grimly. "We've been hit."

———

"The arrow hit the balloon," Xander said. The rest of the troops murmured in assent. "Did you see it?"

Will and the Old Man nodded.

"They'll never make the tower now."

Will looked at his friend. "He's right, Rico. They won't reach the Pulse generator. It's over." He addressed the troops. "Prepare to return to our base."

Xander's eyes were wide. "But we can't just leave them."

The Old Man laid his hand gently on Xander's shoulder. "Even if they survive the crash, they'll come down within the walls of the fortress. They'll be captured immediately. There's nothing we can do for them."

"I won't accept that."

"Do you think I like it? I don't. But we have to face the reality of our situation. There's nothing we can do."

"There is," Xander said, shoving the Old Man's hand away. "We can attack."

There was an audible murmuring from the team. Whether they agreed with him or thought him ridiculous, Xander didn't know.

"Xander, I know you're young, but try to look at this with a mature—"

"I will not abandon my friends."

Will frowned. "We'll have time to discuss this later. But the

Sentry will soon be searching to see if there are other Rebels in the area. We must go."

"No." Xander clutched his useless stunner. "If you won't come with me, I'll go alone."

"Xander, don't—"

Xander shot out from the brush, running at top speed, straight toward the open gate of the fortress.

# THIRTY-ONE

"We're plummeting fast," Daman said. "Is there any way to repair the hole?"

"Sure," Brita said, "if you have some way to climb on top of the balloon."

In other words—no. They would crash to the ground—inside the fortress. If the fall didn't kill them, the Sentry surely would. "There must be something we can do."

"We're close to the tower."

"So? The balloon is falling."

"We could jump."

"Jump?" He peered over the edge of the basket, then down at the ground, which approached at frightening speed. His nausea and dizziness returned. "We'd kill ourselves."

Brita's lips were pressed tightly together. "We're dead either way."

———

XANDER RACED ACROSS THE FIELD. He hoped to get close enough to slip through the open gate before anyone spotted him.

A dozen or so Sentry loitered outside the gate. One of them spotted him while he was still more than a hundred feet away.

But he did not stop running.

Half a dozen Sentry started toward him at once. Fine, Xander thought, let them come. I may not be able to take them all down, but I'll give them a fight they won't forget. At the very least, they'll think twice before they mistreat a "mere" slave.

He ran toward them, shouting at the top of his lungs.

To his surprise, they backed away.

He shouted even louder. Cowardly Sentry, he thought. They outnumber me six to one, and still—

Wait a minute. They weren't just backing away. They turned and bolted, moving as fast as their feet could carry them. He knew he wasn't that frightening.

He slowed, then stopped. He heard something.

The sound of many feet, running.

He turned and saw the ground assault team, all together, a few hundred feet behind him.

They were coming after all. Every last one of them.

Following him. A slave.

A bitter smile crossed his face. Now the Black Sentry would have a fight.

———

"The ground team has begun its attack," Daman said, watching the dramatic tableau from above.

"That's crazy," Brita replied. "Their weapons won't work."

"They're doing it, just the same." He saw the bowman and others who had devoted their attention to the balloon abruptly run toward the front gate. They had a new priority now. The fortress was under attack.

"This could be a break. Most of the Sentry are joining the fight. Only a few are staying behind to watch us."

"No doubt we seem the lesser threat. Since they expect this balloon to crash and kill us."

The balloon suddenly rocked to one side. He fell to his knees. "What happened?"

"We found the tower," she said. "Or it found us."

The gleaming black tower rose beside the balloon. "We seem to be dropping faster now."

"Hitting the tower probably caused another puncture, or widened one of the previous ones." Brita scanned the tower. "At this rate, we should drop by the upper window at any moment. Be ready to jump."

"I—I don't think I can."

"I know you can."

"How can you be sure?"

"Because you don't have any choice." She took his hand and crouched on the edge of the basket, holding a support rope for balance. The instant she saw the top of the large wide window, she jerked him forward. "*Jump!*"

They did. There was glass in the window, but fortunately, no pane. They crashed through and fell to the floor of the room inside, shattering the glass. Shards sprayed all around them. He was cut in a dozen places.

But they were inside.

"Brita? Are you all right?"

She crouched down on all fours, gasping for breath. "Sure. Fine." She had a gash across her forehead gushing blood. He ripped off the sleeve of his tunic and pressed it tightly against her wound. Despite the bleeding, it was not a deep cut.

"Can you go on?" he asked.

"I didn't come this far to give up now." She pushed herself to her feet. He could tell it required some effort, but she didn't complain. He wrapped the sleeve around her head and tied it in the back, creating a makeshift bandage. "Let's find what we came for."

"The Old Man said it would be in the highest room. Let's go this way."

The tower had but a single winding staircase, spiraling upward.

The interior of the tower was like no place he had ever seen before. The floor was made of a white smooth surface, a material he had not previously encountered. The walls were soft and colored, covered with some fine fabric. There were drawings on the wall—paintings, according to Brita—and sculptures, and other creations that served no purpose other than to decorate.

An odd look for a stronghold of the Sentinel, he mused. There was nothing efficient or orderly about it. But it was beautiful.

He wished he could spend more time examining the drawings, but he knew some of the Sentry on the ground must have seen them jump though the window. It wouldn't be long before someone came after them.

For that matter, some of the Sentry might be posted in the tower itself.

At last, they arrived at the top. The corridor ended. There were no stairs or any further means of upward passage.

They walked through a door . . . and entered the most spectacular room he had seen in his entire life.

"It must be here somewhere," he muttered, spinning around. This room, like the corridor outside, was not filled with anything the Sentinel would call efficient or orderly. Beautiful furniture and colorful decorating. Glittering objects, lovely to behold. There was a bed in the far corner—a huge bed. Did someone actually sleep up here? What a life that must be.

"Over here," Brita said.

He ran beside her. In the opposite corner, beside an open window, she discovered a flat table, bigger than his bed at home. On the tabletop rested a strange device encased in a hard metal shell but with visible parts on the exterior, many of them moving, emitting a low hum.

It could only be a Machine.

"Is this—?" Daman asked tentatively.

"It must be. The Pulse Generator."

He removed the red stone hanging from his neck. "Now we must—"

He froze. Cold fingers gripped his neck.

He spun around to face the Acolyte.

"Well, Daman Adkins, you made a commendable effort, I'll grant you that. In a thousand years, no Rebel has come so far as you. The construction of the balloon—that was particularly clever." His eyes narrowed. "But it's over now. Your assault is finished. And your friends are doomed.

# THIRTY-TWO

Xander never fought so hard in his entire life. But if they lost this battle, it would not be because he failed them.

The plain outside the fortress had become a battlefield. The ground assault team—almost fifty of them—swarmed up behind him, racing toward the still-open front gate to the fortress. As soon as they were spotted, the Black Sentry poured through the gate to meet them. He couldn't stop to take an accurate head count, but he knew the Rebels were outnumbered by at least three to one.

The struggle was hard-fought and intense, with fists and clubs and knives. Valiant as they were, he knew the Rebels couldn't possibly hold out for long against such odds. If the stunners didn't come into play, they would eventually lose this battle.

And what was the likelihood that the stunners would be activated? He had seen the balloon go down, had seen it drop out of sight within the high walls of the fortress. He hoped Daman and Brita had survived, but even if they did, the chances that they might make it into the Tower and shut off the Pulse seemed slim. He needed to get inside that fortress to see if he could help. Assuming they were still alive. And if not, he had to recover the Key before the Sentry did.

He heard a harsh whizzing sound overhead. He turned in time to see a Rebel, not five feet away from him, clutch his chest and fall to his knees. A wooden shaft protruded from his chest. Blood seeped from the wound.

He turned his attention to a parapet on the north wall. The man with the bow and arrow had repositioned himself. Having successfully brought down the balloon, he was now slaughtering the ground troops.

Xander fought his way through the Sentry who stood between him and the front gate. Life as a slave might have other drawbacks, but it insured that a young man would learn to defend himself—if he hoped to survive. As a slave, you had to fight for everything.

Another Sentry, a man twice his size, rushed toward him. He ducked, grabbing the Sentry around the legs and knocking him to the ground. They both fell, but the Sentry got the worst of it. He grabbed the man's head and slammed it down on the barren ground. The Sentry's eyes fluttered, then closed.

He jumped to his feet and continued battling his way to the front gate. He didn't kill anyone—he didn't have to. He had learned that a forceful blow to the throat or the chest could quickly bring a man to his knees.

He was perhaps twenty feet away when he saw the front gate start to close. Of course, it was the logical thing to do. Once the gate was closed, with the balloon grounded, the fortress would be virtually impregnable.

Xander rushed forward at top speed. He ignored everyone who stood between him and the gate, weaving and bobbing between them. The gate was open a crack as he approached, barely a foot across. Xander dove forward, launching himself sideways with all his might.

He hit the ground and rolled, squeezing through the opening at the last possible moment.

"Rebel!" one of the Sentry shouted. "Inside!"

He didn't wait for them to come to him. He climbed a nearby ladder and made his way to the parapet. Fortunately, his quarry was focused on the struggle outside and didn't see him until it was too late. He smashed into the bowman, knocking his deadly weapon out of his hands and breaking it into pieces.

The bowman whipped around, his face transfigured by rage. He swung his fist, pummeling Xander on the side of his face. He managed to keep his head together. He flew at the bowman, shoving him back, butting his head into the man's stomach.

The bowman's anger intensified. He brought his fists down at the base of Xander's neck. The pain was intense. He fell to the floor of the parapet.

His opponent saw his opportunity and took it. With an evil grin, the man kicked Xander in the ribs.

He knew one more such blow would take him out of the fight. Permanently. The bowman reared back his boot . . .

At the last possible moment, Xander rolled away. The bowman didn't see the move coming. His boot flew out into the open air, connecting with nothing. The bowman lost his balance and tottered. He whipped his arms around, trying to regain his footing, but it was too late. He tumbled backwards, over the edge of the fortress wall.

Xander tried to grab the man, but he was not quick enough. The bowman fell the full length of the fortress wall, head first. He landed with a sickening crunch.

Xander wiped the sweat from his forehead. His hand came

back covered with blood. He must be hurt, somewhere, but he didn't have time to dwell upon that. The bowman was down, but there were three more Sentry racing up the ladder toward him, determined to make sure he didn't advance any further.

———

Daman shoved the Acolyte away.

"Did you really think that a few children could bring down the Sentinel?" the Acolyte asked, a contemptuous sneer on his face.

"This battle is not over." He was determined to be brave, even if he felt anything but. "The Resistance is attacking the fortress as we speak."

The Acolyte waved his hand dismissively. "I know all about your pitiful accomplices. Fifty Rebels at most. I have more than three times as many Sentry stationed here."

Three times? Could that be true? If it was, they had little hope of success . . . unless they disabled the Pulse.

"You say you know about the Rebels," Brita said. "But that isn't possible. They've only just emerged from hiding."

"Honestly, girl, what do you take me for? I'm the Acolyte of the Sentinel. Do you think it's possible you could do anything the Sentinel wouldn't know about? I've known all along you were coming."

Could this be true? Had the Acolyte been toying with them all along?

"I don't believe you."

"I don't care what you believe, girl. It's true."

"If it's true," Daman said, "why did you let it happen? Why didn't you stop us?"

"Because you had something I wanted." Without warning,

the Acolyte snatched the red stone out of his hands. "And I thought the easiest way to recover it would be to have you bring it to me."

His throat went dry. Had he been nothing all along but a pitiful pawn in the Acolyte's plans?

The Acolyte placed the Key around his own neck. "As the Sentinel's Acolyte, I'm entrusted with the Key for this region. It was a gross failure to allow that traitorous Rebel to steal it from me. My only hope of redeeming myself was to recover it. Thank you, Daman Adkins, for making that possible."

"But—I didn't steal the Key. You couldn't possibly have known—"

"That you had the Key? That you took it from the Rebel and hid it before he was captured? Oh, but I did know. I had it on the soundest authority."

Wordlessly, the Acolyte stepped back, gesturing broadly with his right arm.

A moment later, he detected a movement behind one of the hanging red curtains. The Acolyte's informant emerged, his all too familiar face set in stone.

Mykah.

———

XANDER JUMPED down from the parapet onto the lower landing and grabbed two of the arrows that spilled to the ground when he tackled the bowman. The two Sentry in front saw what was coming, but didn't react in time. Xander put an arrow in each hand and rushed them, piercing each Sentry in the stomach.

Both fell to their knees, clutching their bleeding bellies. Even Xander was taken aback, but he had no time for guilt. There was a third Sentry . . .

Who took one look at what happened to his companions and ran.

He started after him—then came to a sudden stop.

The ground began to tremble.

He knew what it was before he even looked. He climbed back onto the parapet and looked into the field.

Three Silver Sentrymen entered the field of combat, rattling the entire fortress with each step.

He felt his knees weaken. He knew his friends were strong and valiant and dedicated. But they could not hope to defeat these inhuman creatures.

All at once, the field became a sizzling crisscross of blue beams incinerating everything they touched. The fighting continued, but now the Rebels had even more to worry about. Somehow, they had to fight the Black Sentry while dodging the beams of the giant machines.

He knew they could not last long. They could not hope to triumph with those silver monstrosities in the field.

The battle was lost.

Even though he knew it was suicide, he resolved to join the rest of the assault team. He couldn't see any way into the Tower, and if he was going to die, he wanted to die fighting. As he climbed down from the parapet, he spotted two other members of the Sentry, older men, moving rapidly toward the central Tower.

Why were they not joining the fight?

He followed them to the Tower. As far as he could see, there was no entrance, but that didn't seem to stop them.

They paused at the base of the Tower. Xander ducked behind an embankment and watched. One of them scrutinized the wall for a moment, then pressed his hand against two of the tower stones in succession.

To Xander's amazement, a door suddenly appeared.

The two Sentry scurried inside. Once they were out of sight, Xander hurried toward the opening, but by the time he arrived, the door had disappeared again. He tried pushing some of the stones, but nothing happened. No doubt it was not enough to push just any stones—it had to be the same two. But which stones were the right ones?

The cries and shouting beyond the gate told him the battle still raged. The Rebels fought, but they could not possibly last much longer. He had to get inside.

But how?

———

"How could Mykah know anything?" Daman said, gazing at his former friend. "I never told him—"

"You didn't have to," the Acolyte replied. "After your escape from Clovis, your friend Mykah was rather in disgrace. Surely you didn't think we would be fooled by that tiny bump on his head. The penalty for betraying the Sentinel is quite severe. But I gave him one last chance to redeem himself. I told him I would save him—if he told me everything he knew about you and your exploits. Which he did."

Daman glared at Mykah. "Is this true?"

Mykah looked away.

"Once I heard the whole story," the Acolyte continued, "it was easy to piece together what had happened. Mykah spotted the Key around your neck back in Clovis. No one would bother to steal the Key unless he planned to use it. Which meant you would come to Balaveria." He smiled. "It was all too predictable."

Daman turned to Brita. "Run."

They both started, but neither got far. The Acolyte stopped Brita, while Mykah grabbed him and held him fast. Mykah took both of his arms and twisted them behind his back. He tried to resist, but it was useless. Mykah was stronger than he was. He always had been.

The Acolyte approached, his teeth clenched. Without warning, he whipped back his hand and slapped him across the face. "Impudent child. Did you really think you could bring down the Sentinel?"

"I could but hope," he answered, biting his sore lip.

"You've been brainwashed by the babblings of a useless old man. You're fighting for an illusion. A nightmare. Do you really want to live in a world filled with chaos? Where everyone serves themselves instead of the greater good? Where everything is unpredictable?"

"I want a world filled with freedom," he replied.

"Do you really? Do you want to make all those difficult decisions for yourself? Do you think you can? The Ancients couldn't. Don't be misled into thinking their world was some sort of paradise. It was madness. Unhappiness was rampant. Everyone was dissatisfied. Depressed. There was no harmony, no justice. No peace or tranquility. They were traumatized by decisions they were ill-equipped to make."

"They had books," Brita said, trying her best to twist free.

"Books? What good did that ever do them? Books only made people want what they couldn't have. Made them discontented, unhappy. Gave them ideas. The Sentinel's world is a far better place, and if you hadn't been influenced by these Rebels you'd realize that."

"I don't believe you," he said firmly. And he didn't. He didn't know why, but just as surely as he had known anything since this adventure began, he knew that the words the Acolyte spoke were false. "You're wrong."

"It doesn't matter what you think, stupid boy. I'd hoped there might be some chance to rehabilitate you. You're obviously a resourceful lad. The Sentinel could use someone like you. You might've even been an Acolyte one day. But I see now that's hopeless. You must be disposed of as quickly as possible." The Acolyte gripped him tightly by the neck. "And we're not in the village any more. We won't bother with the Ritual of Execution. We'll just kill you."

# THIRTY-THREE

Xander pounded at the stones, trying to recreate the pattern the Sentry had used to open the door to the tower. How many possible combinations could there be? The man had reached high, then low. High, then low. After several unsuccessful random attempts, he tried matching one high brick with all the potential low ones, systematically running through all the possible combinations.

If he had all day, or even a few hours, he'd be able to find the correct pattern. Eventually. But he didn't have that long. He had a few minutes at best. Without weapons, they couldn't hope to win. Soon they would all be killed. He had to get inside before that happened.

He continued pounding at the stones. At last, he heard a clicking noise somewhere on the other side. For a moment, nothing happened, and then all at once, the door reappeared. The stone facade slid back creating a passage just large enough to enter.

He didn't know how long the door would remain open. He jumped through. An instant later, the door swung closed behind him.

Inside, the tower was dark, but not so dark he couldn't see. A central staircase led up and down. He didn't know which to choose. He recalled hearing that the Pulse generator was up high, but he heard loud noises coming from below him. He decided to try that way first.

The staircase twisted and turned so many times he became dizzy. How far down could they travel? It seemed as if he were descending into the bowels of the earth.

At long last, the stairway ended. He stepped through a low portal . . .

And looked out into the most enormous room he had ever seen, even bigger than the cavernous Resistance headquarters. The sides of the room were flanked with huge machines, great noisy wheels and pistons and other gigantic Constructs he couldn't identify. Steam erupted in short bursts, contributing to the overall grayness of the area.

This must be where the Silver Sentrymen are made, he thought. This is what we've come to destroy.

He dropped down from the stairway, keeping an eye out at all times for Sentry. He discovered a lower level just below him. This area was filled with long endless tables, stretching as far as the eye could see.

And the tables were lined with people.

Old people. Gray-haired and bearded people, like the Old Man, some even older. Far older than anyone he had ever seen in Merrindale.

He knew what it must mean. These were the people who had left their village after the Ceremony of Passage. These were the trusting citizens who voluntarily departed, thinking they were headed for paradise.

They were not even doing work that would help their villages. They only served the Sentinel. Building the monstrous Silver Sentrymen.

These were the slaves of Balaveria, the Sentinel's forced labor camp.

They worked with hammers, pounding out sheets of metal, attaching bolts and screws, sanding and polishing. None of them smiled. They didn't even look up as he approached. It was as if they were in another world, apart, lost in a dream. Or a nightmare.

He wanted to talk to them, but the Sentry posted all around made that impossible.

Or at any rate, made it impossible to talk aloud.

Xander told Daman that to tell one slave something was to tell them all. And there was a reason for that. They could talk to one another. Without speaking. With their minds. Many slaves believed that something had happened to his people during the time when the Ancients experimented with the fundamental building blocks of life. They were . . . changed, and not just externally. Perhaps the protuberance on their temples that identified them as slaves also amplified their brains and allowed them to communicate with one another.

Not all the people trapped below were former slaves, but many were. He found one close by and made a connection.

*How can I help you?*

**It's impossible.**

*How can I stop the Silver Sentrymen?*

**Also impossible.**

*My friends have weapons that can help. But they will not function because of the Pulse.*

**The Sentinel's machines work and no one else's.**

Quickly, Xander tried to give his new friend all the details.

*My friends have a Key that will turn off something called a Pulse Generator.*

He could sense the excitement in his new friend's mind.

**If they can shut off the Pulse, your weapons should work—and the Silver Sentrymen will be immobilized.**

He did not understand why shutting off the Pulse would stop the Sentrymen, but there was no time for lengthy explanations. If that was the way to turn the tide of this all-but-lost battle, he had to get up the Tower. He would need help, and he would need to distract the Sentry.

*How can I set you free?*

**By lifting the metal lever. But it is guarded by the Sentry.**

Xander moved his eyes toward the floor. The prisoners' feet were held in place by a heavy iron bar. So long as the bar was down, the slaves couldn't move.

Following the bar across the room, he saw the lever that raised and lowered it. He also saw a Sentry posted beside it.

Unfortunately, the Sentry saw him, too. Xander rushed forward before his opponent had a chance to react. Two quick blows to the chin and the Sentry was down on his knees.

He heard heavy footsteps behind him.

The other prisoners had noticed him. One by one their heads lifted. Gradually, their faces slowly came back to life.

He fought the next Sentry while the prisoners watched. At first, he only heard them in his head, the words of others of the slave class, trying to learn more about him, and eventually encouraging him. They were quiet at first, but as it became clear that this might actually be a chance for release, they began to shout, both aloud and silently, urging him on. When the Sentry collapsed after the final blow, the crowd cheered, creating a tumult that echoed throughout the room.

He whirled, alert for more Sentry, but he saw none. He supposed most available hands were outside fighting the Rebels.

He grabbed the lever and pulled with all his might. It was stubborn, probably typically operated by many men.

**Put your foot on the iron pedal.**

Below him, he saw a pedal, much like he might see on a cart. He pressed his foot down on it and heard a creaking sound.

Now the lever moved more freely, but it was still heavy and required much effort. He clenched his teeth and pulled all the harder. Sweat broke out on his brow, reminding him that he had a wound he had not stopped to examine. His palms grew wet. Blood rushed to his brain. But he kept pulling.

The lever gave way. A tremendous clanging noise split his ears. And then the iron bars rose.

Cheers erupted throughout the room, so loud they almost knocked him off his feet. The tumult ricocheted off the gray walls and sounded as if it might bring down the ceiling. Every prisoner in the room was on his or her feet, clapping, cheering, crying, shouting for joy.

They were free.

———

DAMAN WATCHED the Acolyte withdraw a small grey box from the pocket of his robe. In some respects, it reminded him of Drake's stunners. But he suspected its function was not so humane.

"Did you know that light can kill?" the Acolyte asked, smiling.

"I've seen blue light come from the arms of your Silver Sentrymen."

"Smart boy." He held the gray box high. "This is a laser. It's similar to the devices the Silver Sentrymen use. Smaller than theirs, but more than adequate to eliminate you."

"Spare Brita," he said. "She's innocent. I forced her to come with me. She—"

"Don't bother. Mykah has already told me everything."

Daman glared at his former friend. "How could you? How could you betray the girl you—?" He stopped. He'd answered his own question.

Mykah looked away again.

"That's it?" Brita said. "You're just going to execute us?"

"Well, no." He passed the gray box to Mykah. "This is your final test. Your last chance to prove your loyalty to the Sentinel." He peered down at Mykah intently. "Kill them."

Mykah took the gray box and pointed it at Daman's head.

He considered pleading, begging, reminding Mykah of all they had once shared. But he decided it would be better to die quietly than to die begging.

Mykah's face was stony, fixed. His finger twitched above the firing button.

"Well?" the Acolyte said. "What are you waiting for?"

Mykah swallowed. "It's just . . . Daman once saved my life."

"Does the Sentinel care about that? You swore an oath."

Mykah's outstretched arm trembled. "We've been friends since childhood."

"The Sentinel is your greatest friend. The only friend who matters."

"But—"

"This is your last chance, Mykah," the Acolyte said. "Do this now or you will be cast out of the Sentry, out of the Sentinel's world, forever."

Mykah drew in his breath. His eyes narrowed, and once again he pointed the box.

"Mykah," Brita whispered, "this isn't you. This isn't who you want to be."

"What would you know about it?" he shot back.

"I know what you said. The last time we were together.

Alone. If what you said was true . . . you won't fire that weapon."

"If you don't," the Acolyte barked, "your career is over. Your *life* is over. If you fail me again, you will join the prisoners of Balaveria."

Mykah's face was drenched in sweat. He hesitated, his hand wavering.

"I'm sorry," Mykah said. He clenched his teeth, moved his finger to the button, and fired.

# THIRTY-FOUR

Daman was prepared to die, but he was not prepared for what happened next.

Xander sprang up behind Mykah and knocked him to the floor. The harsh blue beam from the laser shot downward, burning a hole in the floor. The weapon flew out of Mykah's hands and skittered across the floor.

Xander crawled atop Mykah and hit him again, this time square on the jaw. Mykah's eyelids fluttered. He tried to resist, but Xander pinned him down. One more blow from Xander and Mykah's head fell limp against the floor.

The Acolyte started to run, but Daman grabbed the sleeve of his ceremonial robe and yanked him backwards.Before he recovered, Daman retrieved the red Key. The Acolyte snarled and raised his fist, but at that moment Xander started toward him. The Acolyte turned and raced out of the room.

Xander started after him, but Daman held him back. "Our first priority is stopping the Pulse."

He didn't like the idea of letting the Acolyte escape, but they had to shut off the Pulse or the assault team outside had no chance.

He approached the metal box on the raised table. He still had a difficult time believing that this small box was the source of the Sentinel's great strength.

"I have to assume this button is here for a reason," Brita said, pointing.

"No doubt," he answered. "But I'd feel better if we knew what the reason was before we pushed it."

"We don't have time for a controlled experiment." She pushed the button.

The box responded with a click, loud enough to make them all jump. That was followed by a moment of silence, then a whirring from somewhere inside the table.

The same sound the Silver Sentrymen made before they prepared to fire.

"Are we sure this is the Pulse generator and not a weapon?" he said nervously.

"I'm sure," Brita answered. "Of course, it's possible the generator is armed with its own weapons."

"Why?"

"To prevent people from doing exactly what we're doing now."

The box made a sudden popping noise. And then, as they watched, the metal shell rose into the air.

Beneath the shell they saw a fascinating collection of gears and cogs and belts, all making a low melodic hum. Tiny lights flickered on and off. Thin cards inserted into slots lined up on the right side of the device. He heard a ticking noise, sharp and steady, coming from some kind of mechanism in the rear.

"How does it work?" he asked.

"I don't know," Brita replied.

"I don't care how it works," Xander said. "The question is how do we make it stop working."

"There." Brita pointed to a small indentation at the bottom left of the device. There was a small opening, the same size as the red stone.

A keyhole.

Hands trembling, he lifted the Key to the slot and pressed it inside. He heard a tiny click as it lodged in place. Then he gave it a twist.

The humming stopped. The whirring stopped. The ticking stopped.

Brita covered her mouth. "I don't believe it."

"What?"

"I think we did it. I think we actually shut off the Pulse."

He ran to the window behind the table. It gave him a clear view of the battle waged outside. The fighting still raged. Three Silver Sentrymen were in the field, but they did not move or fire their deadly blue beams.

"Xander, can you knock out this window?"

Barely an instant later, Xander tossed a heavy chair threw the opening, shattering the glass.

He put his hands to his mouth and shouted with all the strength he could muster. "Rebels! Use your weapons! *Use your weapons!*"

And they did.

———

DAMAN COULD NOT BELIEVE how well the rest of the struggle went for the Rebels.

Once the Pulse was disabled, the tide of the battle turned for good. Although the Rebels were outnumbered, the Sentry was unprepared for the stunners, and the Silver Sentrymen ceased firing. All the Rebels had to do was press the wired end of the tiny black boxes against an enemy. The boxes made a sharp sizzling noise and their opponents crumbled to the ground, spasming as they fell. They twitched for a moment, then closed their eyes. They were not dead, merely unconscious, but that was more than sufficient to get the Rebels inside the fortress.

Even better, the prisoners of Balaveria, released from their subterranean dungeon, emerged and joined the fight. Although they were weak and unaccustomed to the intense brightness of daylight, their numbers were great. There were far more prisoners than Sentry at the fortress. At that point, the Sentry fought a battle on two fronts—a battle they couldn't possibly win. After the forces on both sides closed in, the Black Sentry deserted in large numbers, scrambling over the walls and ducking out through the gate.

The battle was won.

He and his friends emerged from the tower still in possession of the Key. They found Drake outside. He carried a large pack on his shoulders and appeared to be searching for something.

"Who can tell me where the machinery is?" Drake asked. "Where do they make the Silver Sentrymen?"

"I know," Xander answered. "I've been there."

Xander led Drake and Daman down the subterranean corridor to what was formerly the labor camp of Balaveria. Drake removed a rectangular package from his pack and placed it under the machine.

"What's that?" Xander asked.

"Another experiment of mine," Drake said. "I think it will work. But of course, like everything else, I haven't been able to test it.

"What do you call it?"

Drake carefully slid open a panel on one side of the box. "I call it a bomb." A red light came on, and a pulsing beeping sound emerged. "*Run.*"

They raced back to the surface. Drake told them their time was short, only as long as it would take them to count to two hundred. Daman didn't understand, but he did gather that this was not a good time to be asking questions.

Xander climbed up on the parapet and shouted so that everyone could hear.

"Listen to me! We must leave the fortress! Everyone! Gather at the edge of the forest. But leave now!"

The word spread.

The Rebels raced out of the fortress even faster than they'd arrived. It was a mad rush for safety, for the security of the outcropping just beyond the clearing.

Seconds after they reached safety, a thunderous noise shattered the air. Daman turned toward the fortress and was astounded to see it crumbling before his eyes. The destruction started at the base of the fortress and worked its way up. The stone walls shattered like glass. The tower wavered at first, then tumbled to the ground with a mighty crash, smoke billowing up in its wake.

A huge cloud of fire shot up from the base of the fortress, then slowly subsided. Dust and debris blew around them. He could feel the heat even from where he hid.

Once the smoke cleared, he saw what remained—or more accurately, what didn't remain. The fortress was gone, replaced by an immense rockpile. A useless expanse of rubble.

"Congratulations," he said to Drake. "I believe your bomb worked."

"Yes," Drake answered, but there was no smile on his face, no pride in his accomplishment. "I've taken the first step toward bringing new hope to this world—by reviving the worst fear of the last one."

———

DAMAN HAD NEVER FELT such a rush of joy in his entire life. Somehow, with only the tiniest of chances, they had managed to prevail.

After the dust settled, the Rebels took inventory. Happily, their casualties were light, although the few who were gone were sorely missed. Many Rebels were wounded, but the physic tended their wounds. Few injuries were permanent. The majority would heal in time.

Most importantly, the Pulse had been disabled. The production of the Silver Sentrymen had been terminated. Apparently the protective device that allowed the Sentrymen to function when the Pulse was active caused them to malfunction once the Pulse was gone. The Rebels could now battle the Sentinel and his minions on their own terms, using the weapons devised by Drake and the others.

For the first time in forever, they had a fighting chance.

As twilight fell, the Rebels made their way back to their headquarters. Their ranks had swelled—because most of the prisoners freed from Balaveria had joined them. Few wanted to return to their former villages. They would not be safe there, not while the Sentinel was still in power. And even fewer wanted to risk life on their own in the great forest. They knew the Sentinel's world was a lie and they were anxious to do whatever they could to bring his oppressive reign to an end.

And all of this happened, Daman mused, all these world-shattering events took place, on my birthday. That made him smile. This time, perhaps, the Sentinel was the one who would be winnowed.

As they walked, he noticed Xander ahead of them, walking alone.

He quickened his step. "Xander."

As he approached, he noticed the slight stiffening, the discomfort that came over Xander.

"Yes?"

"Drake told me about everything you did. Leading the troops into battle. Sneaking into the fortress. Freeing the prisoners."

"I did what I could."

"And of course, you made one other achievement of some small importance—you saved my life." He grasped Xander's shoulders, forcing him to stop walking and to look him in the eyes. "And Brita's. You made it possible for us to disable the Pulse. More than anyone else, today's victory belongs to you."

Xander shrugged uncomfortably. "We all helped."

"I just wanted to tell you, Xander . . ." Daman coughed. "To —to tell you that I'm—um—"

"Yes?"

He drew in his breath. "I wanted to tell you that I'm proud to be your friend."

Xander's lips parted.

"I mean, if you'll have me."

"You . . . want me to be your friend?"

He clasped Xander's hand. "You are my friend. You always have been. The best friend a boy could hope for."

———

AFTER NIGHT FELL, Daman and the others reached the cave. Just as he was about to enter, he heard the Old Man calling him. "Daman, could I speak with you for a moment?"

"Of course." They walked for a short while into the forest till they were alone. "What is it?"

"There are things I must tell you. Things you don't know, although I believe you may suspect."

His brow creased. "I don't know what you mean."

"You're a fine boy, Daman. We've been through quite a lot together now, so I feel I can be honest. I'm very proud of you. And I know your father would be proud of you as well."

He beamed. The Old Man's words meant more than he could possibly express. The Old Man was the chief Rebel of the Resistance, the one who'd acquired the Key, the one who'd made it all possible. He still loved his own father, but he thought of the Old Man as a father as well.

The Old Man paused, as if unsure how to continue. "This is a great day for the Resistance. The greatest we have ever seen. But the work has just begun. With the Pulse disabled in this region, we will be able to fight the Sentinel's forces on equal terms—perhaps even better than equal. But what of the rest of this great land? What of the other regions to the east? Someone must disable their Pulse generators."

"That work should be easier. Since we've already done it once."

"That work will be harder," the Old Man cautioned, "because now the Sentinel will be watching for us. For the first time, he knows he faces a real threat. He will stop at nothing to defeat us."

"But once the other generators are disabled—"

"Then someone must fight the Sentinel himself. And that will be the greatest battle of all. So long as the Sentinel rules anywhere, no one will be free. Or safe."

A new voice entered the conversation. "Certainly you are not safe, Old Man."

A dark figure hovered behind them.

Mykah.

His uniform was torn and bloodstained. His face was burned and black. Somehow, Mykah had survived the explosion and followed them back to their headquarters.

But he didn't dwell on those questions immediately. His attention was diverted by something far more immediate. Far more deadly.

Mykah held the weapon the Acolyte had lost in the struggle. The one he called a laser. And it was pointed right at him.

CHAPTER

# THIRTY-FIVE

"Mykah," Daman said, taking a tentative step forward, "the battle is over."

"Not while you still live."

"Mykah, please. It's not too late for you. Join us."

"Join you? You're traitors. Misfits. A member of the Black Sentry doesn't join traitors. He kills them."

The look in Mykah's eyes was frightening. Almost inhuman.

"I thought we were friends."

"You betrayed our friendship, Daman. All you've done is lie and cheat. That's all you've ever done. Steal what isn't yours. Like Brita. Anything you wanted."

Mykah was barely coherent. He wondered if the explosion had damaged his former friend's brain—or if he had just been pushed to the edge by so much disappointment.

"You're a sinner," Mykah continued. "You violated the Sentinel's Laws and Ways. I tried to bring you back. I gave you every possible chance to repent. You and Brita both. But you wouldn't listen."

"Mykah—"

"If you'd done nothing but destroy yourself, that would be

one thing. But you've destroyed me as well. Taken everything that was rightly mine. Ruined my career, my life. I have nowhere left to go."

"You can join the Resistance."

"I'd sooner die. But you'll die first." His finger tightened over the button.

"*Stop!*" the Old Man commanded. He leaped in front just as the blue beam shot forward. The beam hit the Old Man straight on, burning a hole deep in his chest.

"*No!*" Daman shouted. The Old Man fell to the ground.

Mykah lifted his weapon to fire again, but Daman sprang forward, knocking it out of Mykah's hand.

He was enraged. He pushed Mykah to the ground. They wrestled, struggling for control. Mykah rolled on top of him, crushing the wind from his lungs. The world spun around them. He had barely cleared his vision in time to see Mykah's fist barreling down toward his face.

Daman turned his head to the side, catching the blow just over his ear. He returned a blow twice as hard.

His head rang. Breathing became difficult. He felt totally disoriented.

Get yourself together, he told himself. The Old Man was wounded, and if Mykah got free, he'd be next. Then Mykah would make his way into the cave and shoot everyone in the Resistance.

The truth came to him in an instant. Today was his birthday —and just as he had dreaded for so long, he was facing the Winnowing. Against his former practice partner. The friend who, in a hundred sessions, had always defeated him.

He saw another blow headed his way. He rolled away at the last moment, causing Mykah's fist to hit the rocky ground. Mykah shouted and cradled his hand, giving Daman time to pull himself to his feet.

He threw himself at Mykah, trying to knock his opponent down, without success. He barely even pushed him backward.

Mykah landed a solid blow to his stomach. He doubled over, clutching his gut. That was his last chance to strike back—and he lost it. Mykah had the upper hand again.

Dodging the next blow, Daman cast his eyes around for some weapon—a rock, a stick, anything that would give him an edge. But he found nothing.

He tried to run, but Mykah blocked his escape, then hit him again, this time in the neck. While he was crouched over, Mykah kicked him in the face.

He pushed himself back to his feet. He didn't want to fight Mykah. He realized now that he had never wanted to fight Mykah. Perhaps that was his problem in all their previous encounters. But he had to get help for the Old Man. He raised his fists—

Then they both heard the rattle.

The hideous slithering sound emanated from just a few feet behind where Mykah stood.

In the distance, he saw the rustling of leaves that told him a Creeper approached. He turned to run, but before he moved far, Mykah tackled him, knocking him to the ground. They rolled on top of each other, spinning down a leafy incline. Toward the Creeper.

Mykah ended up on top. He raised his fists high, teeth gritted.

"Mykah! It's a Creeper. Get out of here."

"Not until I've taken care of you." It was like Mykah hadn't even heard. His whole mind was focused on revenge.

Daman pushed with all his might, throwing his opponent to the side. "Come with me, Mykah. We need to—"

That's when he heard the most horrible sound of his entire life, before or after. The sound of a Creeper, so close he could reach out and touch it. A Creeper's raspy rattle in his ear.

It was barely a foot away. Its green gelatinous exterior and its grotesque running sores. The hideous lipless salivating maw, so close he could smell its revolting fetid breath.

Its deadly tail circled overhead.

Apparently Mykah was so focused on the fight he hadn't noticed. He raised a fist in the air. "You won't get away from me this time, Daman!"

The Creeper heard the noise. Its long spiked tail whipped up toward Mykah's head.

Without thinking, Daman reached out and grabbed the tail, deflecting it from Mykah. It still managed to strike a glancing blow to the side of Mykah's face. The poisonous spike did not pierce his flesh, but it scraped down his left cheek.

Mykah screamed.

Daman scooped the laser off the ground and fired it at the Creeper. The deadly blue beam struck the creature and it erupted in flames.

The fight was over.

He leaned against a tree, gasping for breath, staring at the smoking Creeper remains. All his life, he'd lived in fear of the Creepers. Everyone in Merrindale had. They could contain them, they could avoid them, but they could not defeat them. In the history of Merrindale, no one had ever defeated a Creeper.

Until today.

On his sixteenth birthday, he had faced the Winnowing, one unlike any that had gone before. And he'd won.

He looked down at Mykah, who lay helpless on the ground. His left eye was clenched shut. He sweated profusely, bleeding in several places.

"I can't see out of my eye," Mykah cried.

He saw that the venom had split Mykah's skin. Even if he

survived, he would have a nasty scar down his face. His handsome appearance was ruined.

"Let me get you to a physic."

"Leave me alone," Mykah spat out. "You've been sentenced to execution by the Acolyte of the Sentinel."

"Oh, Mykah . . ."

"Go ahead, run off with your friends. It won't matter. Wherever you run, I'll find you. I'll never stop looking. I'll chase you till the day of your death. Which will come at my hand."

He stared at the pathetic, blinded wretch who had once been his friend. A dryness in his throat prevented him from speaking. A moment later, Mykah ran away.

He ran to the Old Man's side and cradled his head. The laser had burned a horrible bloody hole in the man's chest, a wound so enormous he knew it could never heal. The Old Man remained conscious, but the light in his eyes was faint.

A few moments later, Brita and Xander arrived. "We heard the noise," Brita said. "What happened?" They both fell to the Old Man's side.

"Mykah," he managed to explain, fighting back tears. "The Old Man took a blast from that evil weapon meant for me." He held the Old Man's head close to his. "You should not have done that," he said quietly. "You should've let me take the shot."

The Old Man slowly shook his head. "No. I had very little time left in any case. You have your entire life ahead of you."

"But the future of the Resistance depends upon you."

"You're our future, Daman. Not me. I knew it the day I met you. You have a most precious Gift, a remnant from the time of the Ancients. One of the three Great Gifts."

"A Gift?"

"Yes. You have the Gift of Knowing."

"You must be mistaken."

"Why do you think you never learned to love the Sentinel,

as Mykah and the others in your village did? Why did you disbelieve what you were told by the Black Sentry, by the Acolyte?"

He stammered. "I . . . suspected it was because I was an evil distrusting person."

"Then why did you believe me? From the first moment we met?"

"I—don't know."

"Why did you believe Drake, and the other Rebels when they told you about the world of the Ancients, about the truth of Balaveria, about the evil of the Sentinel?"

He did not know the answer. But he knew it was true. He had believed them, from the first instant they spoke to him, without even thinking about it.

"For that matter, why did you always fail in your practice sessions for the Winnowing? You're strong and brave and smart. But your heart wasn't in it. Because you instinctively knew that the Winnowing and everything else in the Sentinel's twisted world was wrong."

"But how could I?"

"You have the Gift of Knowing. An instinctive grasp of the truth. Once there were many like you. But the Sentinel has waged war on those with the great Gifts. Now I fear there are very few. Your father had it—"

"My father?"

"Of course. Where do you think you got it?" His breathing was labored. His words came more slowly. "Why do you think your father never accepted the Sentinel's Laws and Ways? Because he knew better." The Old Man took his hand. "You must stay with the Resistance, Daman. They need you. You're a natural leader. Your pure and clear perception of the truth will be apparent to those around you. When you speak, people will listen. When you act, people will follow."

"No one would ever believe me—"

"Think of your trial, Daman. I heard what happened there. You made a daring speech—and people listened. Many agreed —even if they couldn't risk admitting it. Don't be fooled by the bluster of people like the Acolyte and the Sentry. Most people want change. They're tired of being ruled by the Sentinel's tyrannical, inflexible hand."

"But a leader? Me?"

"Think how your friends risked everything to rescue you from the Keep. Do you suppose they would do that for anyone? You are a special, rare individual. As you cross this vast continent, you will gather supporters for the Resistance, people with all kinds of talents and abilities." His eyes drifted briefly to Brita and Xander. "You have already begun to do so. And at last, one day, when your travels are complete, you will be ready to face the Sentinel."

"I couldn't possibly defeat him."

A soft smile played on the Old Man's cracked lips. "I spoke to your father, you know. Back in Merrindale, before I was taken by the Sentry. He once dreamed of being part of the Resistance. But eventually he conformed to the Sentinel's Laws and Ways. At least outwardly. He regretted that decision. And he was determined that you should not make the same mistake. He asked me to give you a message if I saw you again."

"What message?"

"He asked me to tell you"—the Old Man drew in his breath —"that he understood why you helped me, and that he knew you were doing the right thing."

"He did?"

"Indeed, and there was more. He wanted me to tell you that he was very proud of you. And of what you have become."

He felt a catch in his throat. "Did he say anything else?"

"He gave me something. To give to you." The Old Man reached inside his tunic. "He wanted you to have this."

It was the Watch, the ancient timepiece, his father's precious Relic. His most precious possession. And now it was something more. It was a symbol of another time. A time when people governed their own time, when they were free to make their own choices, good or bad.

He felt a distinct itching in his eyes. "I will treasure this always."

"You must act quickly," the Old Man said, so quietly he could barely hear it. "My quest is now yours, Daman. We have slowed the Sentinel, but we have not defeated him. He will try again to build the Silver Sentrymen, perhaps in one of the other regions. If the Silver Sentrymen take hold throughout the Sentinel's empire, resistance will become impossible. And the Sentinel has plans for other monsters even more horrible. You must act now, before that happens. Find the other Pulse generators and disable them. Defeat the Sentinel, and restore the freedom of the people. That is your destiny."

He squeezed the Old Man's hand. "I will try to be true to the task you've given me," he whispered. He glanced up at Brita and Xander. "Given us."

"We all will," Brita echoed.

"We will not fail you," Xander added.

The time for talking came to an end. The Old Man's eyes fluttered closed.

"Does it hurt—very much?" Daman asked.

"No," the Old Man whispered. "I'm past all that. It's not bad, actually. Peaceful. I can rest easy. Knowing you will carry on the work."

"During the Ritual of Execution," he said, "I heard the Acolyte use your real name."

He nodded slightly.

"May—May I use it? Now?"

A smile flickered faintly on his lips. "Yes."

"Thank you. For everything." His eyes brimmed with tears. He squeezed his friend's hand as tightly as he could. "Farewell, Rico Dandel."

The Old Man's head shook slowly. "Till we meet again."

———

DAMAN BURIED HIM AT SUNRISE, at the top of a great hill several miles from the cave where he would not be disturbed. Following his instructions, he and Xander marked the grave with two sticks placed perpendicular to one another.

After they finished, he stood atop the hill for a long while, thinking of all that had happened in such a short time. He could not imagine what lay before them—new people, new discoveries, danger, and perhaps even death.

Drake disappeared on another of his scavenging runs. Will remained in charge. With the slaves from Balaveria swelling their ranks, the Resistance was stronger than ever. Now that the Pulse was disabled, they intended to press their advantage. They would spread throughout the region, fomenting insurrection, enlisting support, until at last they were strong enough to overcome the Black Sentry.

He and Brita and Xander agreed to travel east in search of the other Pulse generators. They would find or recruit more Rebels. They would attack the other power stations. And then, once all the Pulse generators were eliminated, it would be time to unite the growing legion of Rebels and to strike against the Sentinel himself. The legacy the Old Man left them was both frightening—and exhilarating.

He sat on the hill for some while, gazing at the rising sun.

His hand touched the Relic in his pocket and a smile came to his lips.

At last, Brita placed her hand gently on his shoulder. "We should go now."

"The sooner the better," Xander added.

Daman nodded. They gathered together their supplies and provisions and set out to see what lay to the east, certain of only one thing.

Despite everything they had been through, the adventure was just beginning.

# Acknowledgments

I want to thank my early readers, James Vance, Faith Wylie, Tamara Grantham, Sabrina Fish, Savannah Thorne, and Ralph Bernhardt for their insightful comments and advice. This book is better because of you. Thanks also to Jared Pike for his excellent recording of the audiobook.

William Bernhardt

# ABOUT THE AUTHOR

WILLIAM BERNHARDT is the bestselling author of more than sixty books, including *The Florentine Poet*, *The Game Master*, the popular Ben Kincaid and Daniel Pike courtroom novels, and *Nemesis: The Final Case of Eliot Ness*. Bernhardt founded Writer-Con, which hosts writing workshops and small-group retreats, an annual conference, and also offers a newsletter and magazine on Substack. His programs have educated more than three dozen now-published authors. He holds a master's degree in English literature, has won the Oklahoma Book Award twice, and has received the Southern Writers Guild's Gold Medal Award, the Royden B. Davis Distinguished Author Award (University of Pennsylvania), and the H. Louise Cobb Distinguished Author Award (Oklahoma State), which is given "in recognition of an outstanding body of work that has profoundly influenced the way in which we understand ourselves and American society at large." In addition to the novels, he has written plays, a musical (book and music), humor, nonfiction, children's books, biography, poetry, and crossword puzzles. He is a member of PEN International and the Academy of American Poets.